Skitterbrain

by IRENE BENNETT BROWN

Cover by Lydia Rosier

Kerri Bertrand year 1980

I Love you all

SCHOLASTIC BOOK SERVICES
New York Toronto London Sydney Auckland Tokyo

For my daughters,
Melia Elaine and Shana Leigh

No character in this book is intended to represent any actual person; all the incidents of the story are entirely fictional in nature.

ISBN 0-590-30906-4

12 11 10 9 8 7 6 5 4 3 2 1   11   9/7 0 1 2 3 4/8

Contents

On the Farm

Early dawn glowed softly across the harsh Kansas prairie outside the sod house where Larned "Larnie" Moran was just waking up.

Behind their thick lashes, Larnie's grayish-green eyes clouded, and her mouth puckered in distaste as she took in the ugliness of the dimly lighted lean-to where she slept. She rolled off her cot onto the quilt she had kicked off in the night, thinking that never before in all her eleven years had she felt so dowdy and unhappy.

Heaving a deep sigh, Larnie got to her feet and dragged her nightgown up over her head. Her entire being wanted to rebel against getting dressed this May morning of 1875, but she drew on her underdrawers and itchy petticoat and reached for the faded dress that had once been bright blue stripes. Over the dress, which ended in a wide ragged ruffle at her ankles, Larnie tied on a pinafore that was dirt-stained in spite of countless washings with lye soap.

The straw-filled tick on the cot scratched as Larnie sat down to put on her stockings and scuffed, high-topped shoes, and she wriggled angrily. Everything scratched on this awful Kansas farm: her clothes and bed, the gritty dust always blowing about, those awful sandburs and chiggers. There was no end to it!

Her chin jutted out. She wouldn't wait another day to run away, go back to Aunt Helena's in Leavenworth. Leavenworth... Larnie thought in yearning desperation, where folks dressed so fine and lived in comfort.

A frown creased Larnie's forehead. How many times in the past months had she wanted to run away, then changed her mind? Too many! With all the grit everywhere, there was little grit in her. She was a coward. Still...

Larnie bit on her lip to stop its trembling and trudged into the main room of the sod house. At a wash bench inside the door she splashed a precious dipperful of water into a basin and went about washing her hands and face as best she could. She needed no mirror to tell her that the ever-blowing wind and dust had turned her skin rough, and that the searing sun had put freckles across her turned-up nose and cheeks and made her once soft brown hair become sun-streaked and strawlike. And just when she was starting to care how she looked, and wanted so much to be pretty.

A whispery shuffle from the far end of the room immediately diverted Larnie's thoughts from herself. "Mama, don't get up," she cried, turning. "I'll get Papa's breakfast. Right after I milk Bessie. You know Doctor Garth —"

"— said I was to be a loll-a-bed. Save my strength for having the baby," Mama finished. "I think that staying in bed is what makes me feel so weak, Larned."

Mama smiled warmly and waved her hand, but that did not keep Larnie from noticing the bluish circles under her mother's eyes, nor her slow, careful steps. They really should have stayed in Leavenworth. But they hadn't. Mama must have seen the worry in Larnie's face, because her thin arm lifted to give Larnie's shoulder a gentle squeeze.

"You mustn't worry, dumpling, I'll take care. And you'll be happier here on the farm with the baby to play with! Is Papa up and out already?" she asked. She shook her head, her long brown hair rippling on her narrow shoulders. "That windmill."

Larnie's spirits, which had begun to lift at mention of playing with the baby, took a dive. "It seems like he never stops working on it," she grumbled.

"With the best reason there is," her mother said, easing herself into a chair and tucking the fullness of her nightgown in close around her. "Our survival. Papa will finish it before the heat of summer, you'll see. Our very own farm will get off on the right foot with plenty of water for our crops." Her thin face glowed. "Please try to understand, Larned. This is our one chance to be independent, not to count on Helena for every bit of food we eat; the roof over our heads...."

Larnie's face grew warm. She swallowed guiltily. She knew her father's reasons for buying this horrible farm, but it didn't change how *she* felt. It was Papa who didn't like working in Leavenworth as a clerk in Aunt Helena's jewelry shop on Delaware Street, Papa who'd said he felt hemmed in and sissified and too beholden to Mama's sister. Larnie had loved living in Leavenworth, and with all her heart wished she were there still.

A sigh interrupted Larnie's thought. "There is so much work to be done," Mama said sadly. "I wish I could be of more help."

Larnie shook her head in warning. She fastened her thick braids above her wide brow and pulled a

4

flappy bonnet over them. The red satin cherries that had decorated the bonnet one lovely Easter in Leavenworth had been lost from one end of their 360 acres to the other, one at a time. The bonnet had lost its shape and now was good only for keeping the sun out of Larnie's eyes.

"Mama," she said as sternly as she could, "please go back to bed, where you belong." Her mother smiled. Larnie's shoulders drooped. She had tried hard to sound grown up, but she'd failed. She took some dried apples from a crock in the cupboard and headed for the door, stuffing the apples into the pocket of her pinafore. She would munch on them while she did her chores.

Outside, the sun was not all the way up yet and the air was cool. Even so, Larnie noticed beads of sweat glistening on her father's forehead as he struggled to raise his home-built tower over the well. They'd found the well already dug when they bought the farm.

Watching her father, Larnie wished she didn't feel so resentful toward him. How else could she feel, though, with Papa continuously stewing and fuming at her? Couldn't he understand that she wasn't used to farm life, that that was the reason why she bungled so many of the chores he gave her, botching things right and left? Often her father had to leave his work on the windmill to help her correct her blunders. Of course that made him angry, and he would growl at her. "You skitterbrain!" he'd call her.

Papa was a short, stocky man in a blue hickory shirt and brown trousers tucked into scuffed boots. He didn't look at Larnie, but even with his back turned she could picture his dark handsomeness and penetrating blue eyes. Larnie started to ask him if he would like her help with the tower, but her tongue dried against the roof of her mouth and she said nothing.

His old blue army overcoat lay on the ground, and with a sigh, Larnie hopped over it and kept going in the direction of the creek. If Papa had noticed her, he gave no sign.

The little creek, a quarter mile from the house, was drying up with the approach of summer, showing cracked clay and drifts of sand here and there on the bottom. But on the banks the grass was still green among the sparse trees. Here Larnie usually staked out the cow, Bessie.

Larnie bit her lip as she thought about milking. If she could only squeeze out a half cupful more milk this morning it would mean she was getting better at *something*. She moved on toward the creek, wondering why Bessie did not bellow a welcome to her as usual.

As she approached the grassy dip in the land

where she had staked the cow, Larnie felt a stab of genuine alarm. Bessie wasn't there!

At the exact spot where she had staked the cow, Larnie found an empty hole in the earth but no stake. In an instant, her father's husky voice flashed across Larnie's mind: "Skitterbrain!" Plainly, she hadn't driven the stake deep enough into the ground and the cow was off up the creek, out of sight, no doubt dragging the stake at the end of her tether.

Larnie made a half turn in the direction of the barnyard where Papa worked. She pressed her fingertips against her gray-green eyes to stop the tears, dropped her hands, and turned back to look for cow tracks in the grassy, sandy soil. Why did that no-good Bessie have to heap more trouble on her? Didn't she have enough? Larnie walked fast, constantly looking, but Bessie was nowhere to be seen. "So-o-o, boss," she called, "so-o-o, boss."

A long time passed before the realization came to Larnie that Bessie had been loose a long time, perhaps all night, and had gone far. Larnie's steps slowed. Important as Bessie was, should she go home and ask Papa to help her look for Bessie? No, she couldn't ask him. Larnie wiped her moist palms on her skirts and paced, vividly recalling what had happened the day before yesterday at the well. She shivered, remembering.

She'd been bone weary from helping Papa plant corn the day before and darkness still blanketed the homestead when she went to the well for water for breakfast. Most of March and April she and Papa had worked side by side from dawn to dark, readying the fields, getting seed into the ground, whenever he wasn't busy with the windmill.

Still groggy with sleep, Larnie didn't notice that the rope fastened to the bail of the bucket was loose. With faint interest, as though she were someone else, Larnie watched the rope fastened to the crank above the well dance free and the bucket tumble and fall down deep into the dark well.

She realized what had happened and hurried to tell Papa. His voice was quiet, but firm. "Go on down after the bucket, Larnie; there's a ladder." At the fear her face must have shown, he added, "The danger is only in your mind, imaginary foolishness. No harm will come to you. Get on with it, now."

"Papa." She shook her head. "I can't go down inside the well. I'd be too afraid. Please don't make me."

Her father's eyes turned a sharper blue, his face turned red. "If I ever teach you anything worthwhile," he said flatly, "it will be to face up to your troubles, make good of your mistakes. I'm sorry, girl, at times it will take real gumption, a lot of courage, but you can do it."

Larnie relented. But her insides were aquiver as she looked down into the well and saw that it was blacker than midnight. Her eyes strained to see the ladder, a single cottonwood limb with short cross poles fastened to it, going down inside the well. According to Mama, it was for going down to rid the water of dead toads and such. Shivering with fear, Larnie started down. The steps were shaky and old, and her lantern, hooked on the crank handle above, shed only a dim light on the upper part of the well.

She inched downward, a forked stick tightly gripped in one hand, and remembered an old fear she had had when she was small. For a long time she had believed that demons lived in wells because whenever she hollered down, the voice that hollered back sounded nothing like her own voice.

It was easy to believe in the demons again. Larnie felt weak. She trembled so much that she could scarcely hold on to the clammy sides of the well, the narrow steps.

In what seemed hours later, she finally reached the bottom. When she looked up, a sharp cry escaped her. The circle of light above, the opening to the well, looked so small! Anxious to be out, Larnie fished around furiously in the five-foot deep water until the forked stick at last caught the bail of the bucket.

Afraid that a step might give way, that she would fall and drown, Larnie climbed carefully up and out of the well. With the recovered bucket sloshing water, Larnie reeled to the house.

She left the bucket of water on the bench inside the door, ran to Mama's bed and lay down stiffly beside her, unable to cry or speak. Finally, in a sudden burst of wrenching sobs, she told her mother everything.

"Papa wouldn't care if I'd drowned," she sobbed. "All he thinks about is this farm. He makes me work like a boy, or a mule. He doesn't care about me. He's forgotten I'm a girl."

Larnie looked up at Mama's face and saw that she was smiling through a few tears of her own. "Now," she said, hugging her close, "that isn't true. Papa wants you to be a whole person, to grow up to be a strong, self-reliant woman. That's all. You see, Larned, it's partly my fault. You being our only child has made me keep you much too close to my skirts. You're spoiled, honey, a nearly helpless little dumpling, now. Papa's right. In the long run, you'll see."

*   *   *

Larnie stopped pacing abruptly. No, she

wouldn't ask Papa to help her find Bessie, but she would go back for their mule, Sunflower. She didn't like riding the mule, but doing so would help her go farther in less time. It looked as if her search for Bessie would take a while.

With both hands clutching at her skirts, Larnie hurried home, hoping that she could get the mule out of the barn without her father's seeing her. How sick she was of being called a skitterbrain!

As Larnie slipped around the corner of the barn, she saw her father just disappearing into the house. With a little sigh of relief, she darted into the barn. The almost white mule, splotched with cream-colored spots, dozed in her stall. She had recently taken to starting fights with Bessie, the brindle cow, biting and kicking, so Larnie let them take turns spending the night in the barn.

"Sunflower, up!" Larnie said, clicking her tongue. Nothing happened. She kneeled and hauled at the cheek strap of the long-eared animal's halter and slapped the mule's hip at the same time. "Get up, lazy," she pleaded. "We've got an awfully important chore ahead of us. Up, Sunflower." At last, the mule slowly unfolded.

"Good girl, nice mule." Larnie stroked the mule a moment, then took the old bridle from the peg on the wall and with luck got the headstall over the mule's head and the bit into her mouth. She tossed a square of blanket up on the mule's back in place of the saddle they didn't have, and led Sunflower from the barn and around to the back.

Larnie wished she could mount Sunflower with at least a little ease and grace. It seemed to her that the mule always grew taller just when she had to mount. After considerable hops, leg flings, and hauling with her elbows, Larnie was astride. She pulled the ragged ruffle of her dress as low as possible down over her legs. With a weary sigh, a squeeze of her knees, and a rusty-sounding hee-haw from Sunflower, they were off at a run.

She would stay close to the creek, Larnie decided, because Bessie would most likely meander along where the grass was greenest. Still, that cow could be anywhere.

For some time Larnie jolted along on Sunflower, seeing no sign of Bessie. The wind from the south picked up, swirling and moaning through the grass, erasing the cow's faint tracks, and adding to Larnie's worries over the missing animal.

What if she couldn't find Bessie? Panic mushroomed inside Larnie as she rode along, recalling an incident that took place at Aunt Helena's not long before they left Leavenworth, when Dr. Garth had come to see Mama.

Larnie had been sitting in the window seat in Aunt Helena's dining room, her attention deep in a copy of Godey's *Ladies Book*. "Little pitchers have big ears." Mama's whisper, referring to the possibility of Larnie's eavesdropping, came suddenly from the next room.

Larnie promptly dropped the magazine and tiptoed quickly to crouch outside the door to the sitting room, where she heard Dr. Garth bark tenderly at Mama, "You have no business having a baby until you fully recover from that bout of pneumonia you had last year, Alice. You're not strong enough. But if you will stay in Leavenworth, where I can look after you, we will manage. You cannot go off to that godforsaken farm with Wint."

Mama answered in a voice that was quiet but firm, "I know you want what is best for me and the baby, Dr. Garth, and I appreciate it. But I must be with Winton, and this is his last opportunity to be a farmer. Because of the grasshopper plague last year, a lot of folks are giving up and selling their farms cheap. This day has been a long time coming for us, and we are going. Wint, Larned, and I. We'll be fine, and so will the baby."

Dr. Garth had growled, finally giving in. "Count on having the baby against the odds, if you will. But don't count on nourishing the infant yourself, Alice, after it is born. For your sake, and the baby's, you have to have a milk cow. You get Wint to take one with you from here. Milk cows are as scarce as hen's teeth out there on that lonely prairie."

Larnie remembered, as she urged Sunflower to move faster, that Mama herself had picked out the handsome brindled cow with golden horns and a large black crescent mark on the left shoulder of her brown-and-black-striped body. Bessie. For the baby, the sleek cow was a matter of life and death. Bessie was more valuable than gold.

Where was Bessie?

The Wide Horizon

The sun was well up, warming the blowing wind. Larnie's eyes studied every direction as she rode, following the creek. Nowhere on the flat, grassy prairie did she see anything that resembled a cow or any other creature.

Taking in the barren land made Larnie remember a comment she had read once about this part of Kansas: "A person can look farther and see less...." It was true. The bright sunlight hurt her eyes, but as Larnie squinted she realized that there were no trees, no rocks or anything pleasant to look at except along the creek. To the north, east, and west lay the wide, bleak horizon. But there was no sign of Bessie.

After a while, Larnie thought she heard voices. Was it just the wind? They had no close neighbors. She halted Sunflower and listened. It was men's voices ahead. Maybe they had Bessie with them, or at least had seen her cow. Larnie lifted her chin and caught her lower lip between her teeth. She did not like the idea of approaching strangers without having Papa along, but she had better do it. She nudged Sunflower with her knees. "Get up."

Larnie strained to look as far up the creek as she could, hoping to spot the people she had heard talking before they saw her. In the water under a leafy, overhanging shrub, she saw something white. All at once the scene came clear; Larnie clapped a hand over her eyes, her face grew hot. Those were two cowboys there in the creek, taking an early morning bath with nothing but their hats on!

She had forgotten until now that Papa said their new farm was a few miles west of a cattle trail leading up from Texas and on to Wichita, Kansas, the Texas Trail. "Larned Louella Moran, you're not about to talk to naked cowboys," she told herself. With a nervous tug at Sunflower's reins, Larnie pulled the mule away from the creek and jogged along fast without a backward look.

When she had ridden more than a mile in an angle from the creek and was three or four miles from home, Larnie heard what she believed might be the faint bawling of a cow to the east. She listened, her heart in her throat, then she urged Sunflower into a bone-jarring gallop. The bellowing grew louder and multiplied. With sudden, sharp disappointment, Larnie realized that she was not hearing a single cow, but many.

Before long she could hear men shouting, "Hi-ah, hi-ah," from far away; 'hi-ah, hi-ah." Somewhere ahead, hidden from her view, must be the cowboys' cattle herd.

Larnie wavered. Should she go on, or should she turn back? She slowed her mule to a walk, glanced back over her shoulder and saw that for some time she had been riding up a gradual swell in the land. Topping the grassy knoll at last, Larnie caught her breath. On a second knoll in the distance she saw cows. Milling, bellowing, and hooking horns with one another, they were being rousted up from their bedground, sending puff-clouds of dust into the morning sky.

Larnie stared at the huge, rippling brown blanket of cattle. Then, from the corner of her eye, she noticed a single cow, closer at hand, loping with arrow-straight determination toward the gigantic herd. Bessie. If Bessie got mixed into that herd of thousands of wild Texas beef cows, they would never see her again. "No!" Larnie screamed without thinking. "Bessie, wait! Go, Sunflower, go!" Another scream tore from her throat, and Larnie jabbed her heels hard into the mule's sides. It was like setting off a volcano. The mule bunched and erupted under her and Larnie was sent flying through the air. The hard ground reached up and smacked the air from her lungs, racked her bones, and ended her thought.

The sun hot on Larnie's face brought her to. She lay quietly with her eyes closed, listening to a voice saying over and over, "That no-good Bessie, that no-good Bessie..." It was several seconds before Larnie realized that the mumbling came from her own dry lips.

"Huh. Huh, huh, huh," a strange voice laughed suddenly.

Larnie's eyes flew open. She lay still and wondered if she was dreaming.

Looking down at her was a boy about eight years old, whose tattered overalls and shirt weren't just dirty, but were shiny and stiff with filth. His hair was the color of muddy sand and was sort of whipped to a peak on his head, as though by a tornado. Large ears stuck out from the sides of his dirty face and his eyes were a pale blue. Not only was his mouth turned up in a grin at Larnie's predicament, but brown tobacco juice stained the corners.

"My cow. Where is my mule? Who are y-you?" Larnie stammered. "Where'd you c-come from?" She rolled over, made it to her knees, and slowly rose to her feet, feeling as if she had been struck by a train. She brushed herself off. "Have you seen my mule, Sunflower? I've got to get my cow, quickly."

The boy jerked his peaked head toward Sunflower, who was standing a few feet away, brown eyes staring back at the boy and Larnie quizzically. "I'm takin' her," the boy announced flatly, still grinning.

"You're what?" Larnie shook her head to clear it. "What did you say?"

"I said I'm takin' the mule." Without another word the boy vaulted astride Sunflower, took up the reins, and they loped away.

Larnie stared, her mind numb with disbelief. A few seconds passed before she staggered after them. "No! Please. You can't! This is stealing. Bring my mule back. Oh, no!" Larnie snatched up her battered bonnet and the dried apples that had spilled from her pinafore pocket. She ran after the boy. "You can't take my mule!"

As she ran, Larnie's dizziness faded and she could see more clearly what was taking place ahead of her. Beyond the boy, riding away fast on Sunflower, was the cattle herd, the point of it now stringing out north toward Wichita. Off to the side and ahead of the herd was a covered chuck wagon that looked like a rolling, dirty gray loaf of bread. Miniature-sized cowboys on horses rode at the ragged edges of the enormous, dust-raising herd.

Larnie saw that the main part of the herd was still milling about. While she watched, the side of the herd opened slightly to swallow into it the brindled cow that had reached the herd at last. Bessie.

A dry sob sounded from Larnie's throat, and she slumped to the ground. It was useless, now, useless. Bessie was gone forever. Their mule had been stolen. Papa would—If ever the time was right to run away to live with Aunt Helena in Leavenworth, it was now.

Papa thought she was a skitterbrain for losing a bucket down in the well. What would he think when he found out that she had lost Bessie among thousands of wild cattle that were being driven to Wichita to sell? And that, no matter that it wasn't her fault, Sunflower had been stolen?

Larnie was sickeningly aware that with every second she sat there alone on the prairie, the distance between her and those two animals was growing. But she did not want to do anything about it. What could she do? Nothing.

She desperately wanted to forget everything that had happened this terrible morning. She wanted to start walking toward Leavenworth. Papa was wrong to bring them here. If she did go to Aunt Helena, maybe the two of them could persuade Papa to come back to the city in time for Mama to have her baby there.

But even as she thought these things, Larnie

knew there was no hope. Papa and Mama were like happy newlyweds about the farm. As Papa kept repeating, "Come drought, grasshoppers, or ten-cent corn, we're staying. This is *our farm*."

They wouldn't leave. Her mother would have the baby on that prairie farm. From the way Mama talked to Papa in her low, private voice, the baby was due any day. Once born, the tiny human being couldn't live long without nourishment.

She had to go after Bessie, there was no choice. Larnie got to her feet. She had covered a good six or seven miles this morning. She was closer to the herd, and the boy on her mule, than she was to home. It wouldn't be easy to catch up on foot. But if she could someway get back their cow, Bessie, and maybe Sunflower, too, wouldn't Papa be pleased and proud of her? Perhaps the bad feelings between them would then be ended for good. . . .

A long, quivering sigh shook Larnie. She drew her shoulders up, bit into a dried apple slice, and fell into a trot behind the fast-moving herd, which seemed to be at least a mile ahead of her.

"All right, Larned Louella Moran," she mumbled around the apple in her mouth, "let's get going. And before the sun gets any hotter."

She felt foolish, talking out loud to herself. But

her heart was heavy and talking helped to ease her sadness. "I think it's about thirty miles or so from our farm to Wichita," she panted into the great emptiness around her. "At Wichita, Papa said, the Texas cows are loaded on a freight train and shipped east to the packing plants in Chicago. Now what you must do, Larned, is catch up with that boy and somehow get back your mule. Ride on fast, then, to that big herd and tell the cowboys to get Bessie out of it for you. No matter what, you can't let Bessie get shipped away east!"

An hour passed, and still Larnie could not catch up with the herd nor with the boy. Another hour went by. Larnie's enthusiastic trot had long since slowed to a dogged walk. She forced her thoughts away from the impossibility of her task and pinned her attention instead on the billowing dust cloud ahead. And she kept going.

There was little to relieve the boredom. Once an antelope bounded along east of the trail and an hour or two after that she watched a snake slither away through the short buffalo grass while she stood frozen with fear.

Each hour she straggled on might have been a day. Time became a thing with no beginning, no end. If she could only fly, Larnie's dazed mind reasoned, she could catch up with the herd in a few minutes, and this awful hurting weariness in her legs would stop.

Larnie reached up and pushed her bonnet back to let it hang by the ribbons on her shoulders. The wind cooled the damp places at her temples and throat, but the sand in it stung her flesh. Larnie squinted and saw the brown dust cloud etched against the blue sky, far, far ahead.

Why couldn't she get close? If only they would slow the herd down, or stop, or something. It would give her a chance to catch up. She supposed, coming all the way from Texas, they wanted to hurry these last few miles at the end of the trail. It made things worse for her.

It was so hot.

A tear started, then dried on her cheek, and Larnie swallowed back the rest. Her glance returned to the sandy ground underfoot, chewed up by the cattle hooves. Her petticoat was a hot, wretched misery, but she did not take it off, alone though she was. She had never gone without a petticoat, or two or three, in her life.

Plodding on, Larnie weaved drowsily over the nearly barren sand. In spite of the apples she nibbled on from time to time, her stomach was a tiny hurting knot. She had had no breakfast. Nor had she fixed breakfast for Papa. She'd promised Mama she would....

By now, Larnie reasoned with an ache in her chest, both Mama and Papa would know she had not come home with Bessie. Papa would have checked this morning at the creek, seen that the cow had gotten loose and, if the wind hadn't destroyed all traces, that she'd gone after Bessie. He must have been very angry, but he would go back to work on his windmill, watching angry-eyed for her arrival home with Bessie.

No, Papa would come after Bessie, too, knowing the milk cow's importance, Larnie argued with herself. Maybe Papa wasn't far behind her. She'd be so glad to let him take over this awful chore. Larnie looked back, but saw nothing but the huge empty prairie.

As she continued on, her eyelids grew heavy and felt as if they were lined with sand. Her feet in her worn-out shoes were like leaden stumps. She had to rest. Larnie slipped to the ground and sat with her arms around her knees, her head low. The sun was broiling.

Behind her closed eyelids Larnie could see Aunt Helena's cool, lovely, vine-covered brick house. She, Larned, was walking in the shady street and then up Aunt Helena's front steps, Mama and Papa close behind her, smiling. Aunt Helena answered Larnie's knock wearing her silver-gray silk dress. "Aunt Helena, we're home!" Larnie announced. "We've come home to have our little baby, we've come home to stay!"

It wasn't true. It was only the imaginings of her

sunbaked mind. Larnie lifted her head and looked up into the sky. Two buzzards were circling above her. "Oh, no," she whispered. "Don't think I'm dead. See, I'm moving." Larnie jumped to her feet and waved her arms. "See there, I'm far from dead."

She brushed the sand from her ragged skirts, pulled her flapping bonnet back up to shade her face, and kept walking north. When she looked again, the buzzards were gone.

Daylight, too, was leaving. When she noticed the reddened sky to the west, whimpers of alarm sounded in Larnie's throat. How far from home was she? Miles and miles, probably — much too far to reach home again before night. Where was Papa? Why hadn't he caught up with her? She didn't want to be alone on the prairie after dark. What would she do?

Larnie choked back her fear and kept walking. She would keep moving, she decided, as long as she could take a step. Then she would simply lie down on the ground and rest. In the morning, first thing, she would catch up to the herd, get Bessie, and be on her way home again. She'd probably meet Papa, coming for her. A deep sigh escaped Larnie. That's how it would be....

At first Larnie could not believe her tired eyes when they picked out what looked like a fringe of trees ahead. She stared a moment, then hurried her steps. They were really trees, tall, leafy cottonwoods. Larnie broke into a run. The trees would be a shelter, a place to rest. She would not have to sleep on the open prairie.

When Larnie reached the cottonwoods she discovered that they bordered a broad, shallow river. There were endless cow tracks, horses' hoofprints, cigarette butts, and cow droppings on the riverbank. But there were no other signs of the Texas cow herd and its drivers. Larnie's spirits sagged. The herd was well ahead of her, across the river and on the way to Wichita.

This was the Ninnescah River, she guessed, from Papa's mention of it. She'd heard him say there were three streams between their farm and Wichita — the Ninnescah, the Cowskin, and the Arkansas. The still water looked cool and inviting. Larnie felt the urge to walk straight into it to cool her sun-hot body, clothes and all. She started forward, smiling. Then a sudden movement on the other side of the river made Larnie's breath catch. She stopped.

Close to a leafy cottonwood that had toppled into the river was her white mule, Sunflower, and the dirty, gnomelike boy.

Night on the Ninnescah

Larnie slipped behind a tree to watch. Near the opposite shore, the boy stood in shallow water, bathing Sunflower's right foreleg. Papa's mule was lame! No wonder she had caught up to the boy! The thieving rascal must have pushed poor Sunflower too hard, trying to get away, and then had to stop when the mule's leg got bad.

Stealing Sunflower was wicked enough, but causing the animal to go lame — she would like to tell the brat what she thought of him! Larnie thought for a moment. She would go downstream, cross the river where he couldn't see her, and then...

Larnie slipped along from tree to tree, and, reaching a likely spot, quickly removed her shoes. She rolled up the legs of her underdrawers, hoisted her skirts, and with her shoes in her hand waded into the river. The water was surprisingly warm. She made her way slowly, her heart in her throat, afraid that any second the boy would look in her direction.

He didn't. Not even for the time she walked high and dry across the sandbar in the middle of the river. Finally Larnie reached the other side, and an eternity seemed to pass before she came quietly up behind the boy in the water. "You've hurt my papa's mule," she said, unable to remain silent for a moment longer.

She gasped and jumped back as the boy spat tobacco juice in her direction. He gave her a weak-eyed glance. "Aint' hurt bad, just pulled a li'l old lig'ment in her leg. Be all right by mornin'." He threw back his head and with careful aim sent a second brown missile to land in the sand near Larnie's bare toes.

"You stop that filthy spitting at me," she cried, fighting the urge to heave her shoes at his head. "I am taking my mule back, right now."

The boy snickered his disdain. "Ain't your mule no way. I took her. She's mine now."

Larnie could scarcely breathe. How was she to handle this — this good-for-nothing boy, how could she make him give Sunflower's reins to her? She started forward, considered the boy's husky arms, his strong build, and stopped. He might be younger than she, but there was little doubt he was stronger. Larnie considered; she was older, wasn't she? Smarter, then? She would have to use her brains to get the best of him.

She walked a short distance upstream from the boy and, finding a clear pool, cupped her hands into it and drank thirstily. She waded around for a time, thinking, but always keeping an eye on the boy as he continued to bathe Sunflower's leg. "Don't let her drink too much water," she said, "she's still my papa's mule."

The boy looked up at her, disgust written across his grubby face. "Why're y'all standin' there like some ol' whooping crane? There ain't no way you can get this mule away from me. Ain't no use tryin'."

Close to tears, Larnie protested. "I have to have the mule. I have to go on after Be — "

"Might as well shet your mouth 'cause I'm keeping this here mule," the boy interrupted. "It ain't none of your never-mind, but I'm trying to catch up with Jeru Hunter. Been tryin' since Injun Territory. I ain't et much, ain't slept much, and I'm plumb wore out. With this mule I got a chance."

"But why do you have to catch up with this — this Jeru Hunter?" Larnie asked. "Who is he?"

The boy scratched his dirty blond hair. "Jeru Hunter is trail boss of that herd that went through here today, that's who. I'm joinin' up with his outfit, if'n I can ever catch up with 'em."

Larnie's heart beat fast. "Then Jeru Hunter is the man I need to see, too." She slumped to the ground, suddenly too weary to stand. Rubbing her sore feet gently, she went on, "Our milk cow, Bessie, got mixed into that man's cattle herd. I have to get our cow back as soon as possible, because my mother is going to have a baby anytime."

The boy snorted. "You won't have no luck pullin' that fib on Jeru Hunter. Them cowboys hear that windy fifty times goin' up the trail. Sodbusters, farmers are always tellin' the cowboys that their stock got mixed in with the herd, so's to git free critters." The boy laughed and wiped at the tobacco juice that dribbled out onto his lip. "Tried that whopper myself, but it never worked. They got brands on those cattle. They know whose is whose. They did give me a calf a time or two, that couldn't keep up." He shook his head, and an old sadness came into his eyes. "My pa always ate 'em."

Larnie shrugged. "I'm not lying, I'm not telling a windy. It's the truth. I just have to get my cow, and I don't have much time. My mama — "

"Now renegade Comanches," the boy interrupted, "stampede the herds. Then they gather up the scattered cows for theirselves. That's the best way of doin' it."

Larnie glared at the boy. She could not convince him with words. Wasn't there any way she could get Sunflower away from him and go on after Bessie? Larnie stood up.

The boy eyed her suspiciously. His hair fairly bristled with defiance as he led the limping mule from the river onto the sandy shore.

"Don't try nothin'," he warned Larnie. "It wouldn't work. I've whupped fellers twice my size, to say nothin' of gals. Wouldn't bother me none to — to scalp you, even. I aim to be a cowboy. Ain't nothin' stopping me."

Larnie watched him tie Sunflower to a cottonwood trunk. The mule began to pick at the clumpy grass beneath the tree. Frustration grew inside Larnie, adding to the hunger and weariness that already was almost more than she could bear. Maybe, if she were more friendly...She studied the boy's ragged back, and then asked in a thin voice, "What's your name?"

"Buzzard," came a mechanical answer, then the boy jerked around and frowned at Larnie.

She was too surprised to speak for a moment. "B-Buzzard? That's not a name for a human being."

"Well, it's the one my pa give me," he snarled. "It's Buzzard. Buzzard!" He turned his back to her, stooped, and began to break small sticks into a pile. He took flint and steel from his pocket and in minutes had a rosy flame licking up from the sticks.

Larnie looked across at him, squatting in the twilight shade of the cottonwood before the tiny glowing campfire. "Do you have food?" she asked hopefully. "I have a few dried apple slices. There is water. We could — "

Buzzard stood up, threw her an anxious look, then growled, "Eat your own durn apples on your way back." He jabbed a grimy thumb in a southerly direction.

Hot tears stung in Larnie's eyes. She gulped. "I have a duty to my papa and mama, and to a little baby who could be getting born right now. I can't go home! Not without our cow, Bessie, and not without Sunflower."

Buzzard grinned at her and patted Sunflower's shoulder. "You bawl-baby girl. Stick aroun' if you're that dumb. But be ready fer me to split that ratty hat you're wearin' with a tree limb. I could. Anytime I get the notion."

She watched him sit down on the ground, nudge his back against the tree, and begin to eat some dirty crumbly biscuits from the brown skin pouch.

Larnie realized that she was as scared as she was angry. But she would not give this boy a hint as to how scared she was. She would stay glued to the sand where she sat, like part of the earth. Something was bound to happen. Buzzard would have to move away from Sunflower for more wood, or he would fall asleep, or something. She would get Papa's mule away from him!

Taking a dried apple slice from her pocket, Larnie wiped it on her sleeve to rid it of dust and began to nibble, almost choking when she tried to swallow. Twilight melted into darkness.

Buzzard's thin face in the light from his small fire looked ghostlike. Larnie shivered and curled up on the warm sand. Her eyes ached and her body felt like mush, but she would not go to sleep. She couldn't forget Buzzard's threat to bash in her skull. But above all, she meant to outlast him in staying awake.

After a long while, Larnie's arm grew numb from the weight of her head. She turned on her other side, so she could still keep an eye on Buzzard, and pillowed her head on her other arm. Longingly she thought of the big, white, lace-trimmed pillows she had snuggled into on her four-poster bed at Aunt Helena's. How long ago that seemed now.

Even her makeshift bed of cottonwood limbs at the farm was a treat compared to this, she thought, twisting about to ease her discomfort. The farm. She had been gone from the farm an entire day. Why hadn't Papa come looking for her? Was the windmill really more important to him than his own daughter? Wouldn't he want to help find Bessie?

Or had something happened — something bad — to keep Papa at home? Larnie stiffened as a picture flashed across her mind... Papa falling, falling, the well caving in on him. She writhed, her chest hurt, and she bit her lip to keep from crying out.

Maybe Papa couldn't leave Mama because the baby had come!

"Please, dear God," Larnie prayed under her breath, "don't let anything bad happen to my mama and papa, or the little baby. Don't let Papa fall into the well; I don't want him hurt. Don't let the baby come yet, either. Help me get home with Bessie in time."

Larnie watched Buzzard's fire die to nothing. To the west of them a coyote or wolf howled, causing Larnie to feel lonelier than ever. As long as she had to be here, she decided, she was glad the boy was here, too. This was not a place she'd want to be alone without a single other human close by. Still, as soon as she felt sure Buzzard was sleeping soundly, she intended to take her mule and ride north after Bessie.

Larnie wriggled fitfully in the sand in an attempt to keep herself awake. Time and again her eyes snapped open to look in Buzzard's direction. His eyes, owl-like, shone back at her. At last, in spite of her struggles, Larnie fell into an exhausted, dreamless sleep.

She awoke suddenly, much later, shivering with cold, and looked around her. The river shone silver in the moonlight. Only the cottonwoods remained dark, whispering in the wind. Larnie lay scarcely breathing, listening for some sound from Buzzard. He was snoring.

After another moment, she eased herself to her feet. She hesitated, but when Buzzard did not stir, she tiptoed, step after careful step, toward the spot where he slept and Sunflower was tethered. At last she reached them. As she looked down at Buzzard curled by the black remains of the fire, he moved slightly and his thumb went straight into his mouth. Larnie stifled a laugh. Mean and tough, was he? Well, not altogether. How the boy would hate her if he knew what she had seen!

Stepping around him, she reached out a hesitant hand to stroke Sunflower. "Easy. Easy," she said softly. The mule shifted on her feet and raised her head, but made little sound. "Good mule," Larnie murmured. Her fingertips traveled along the rope until she found where it was wrapped around the tree. She held her breath as she undid the knot, and then the rope was free and clasped tightly in her hand. "Come," she whispered, "come, Sunflower."

A million stars and the early-summer moon made the night nearly as light as day. Larnie hoped desperately that Buzzard would not wake up. If he should, he would have no trouble taking Sunflower away from her again. Larnie gnawed at her bottom lip and was glad for the sandy ground that muffled the sound of her footsteps, and the mule's.

Leaving the river and the trees, she took a moment to look cautiously back over her shoulder. There was no movement behind her. Buzzard still slept then, she decided. She continued on, and when she looked a second time, there was still no sign of Buzzard following her and Sunflower. Larnie sighed in weary relief.

Larnie stumbled along for several hours, leading the mule, feeling more asleep than awake. Her nose told her that she was still in the path of the cattle herd, and she did not worry that she would become lost in the dark.

Then the night was past, and before long, full daylight had come. Once or twice she thought she could make out a dust cloud far ahead to the north. But the brown cloud could be a swell in the land, she decided, squinting, or a mirage. Or it could be Jeru Hunter's cows, with Bessie among them, she thought, quickening her steps.

Larnie noticed that Sunflower hardly limped at all this morning. As for herself, she felt like something dead. Her decision was made. "Whoa," Larnie mumbled, halting the white mule. With an effort she got herself up on Sunflower's back. "If you start limping bad again, I'll walk," she promised the animal with a pat. "I won't make you run until I'm sure your leg is fine. Although," Larnie grated to herself, "I'd give my heart, almost, to reach that herd fast."

As she rode, Larnie mused about Buzzard. He reminded her of a boy she had gone to school with in Leavenworth, Dud Chester. Dud was a lot like Buzzard, although maybe not quite so dirty. On the front wall of their large, well-ordered schoolroom had been a hand-lettered sign which read, *TIME IS PRECIOUS, WE RUN ON TIME*. Clearly she remembered the morning Dud came to school late, still in pain from a cruel lashing his father had given him for some minor trouble he had caused. Dud had attacked that poster with his jackknife, had hacked it to shreds. Before the teacher could stop him, Dud had destroyed most of the students' drawings of autumn leaves that decorated the room.

Remembering Dud Chester made Larnie feel sad. She shook her head. It wouldn't surprise her if Buzzard had a father like Dud's. Considering the name he had given his son, he couldn't be a kind person.

Larnie's thoughts returned to that sign in the schoolroom, before it was ruined. "Time is precious," she whispered in the broad, open plain. It was — very precious — and too much had gone by with her still no closer to Bessie.

The Wolves

There was no sound to keep Larnie awake as she traveled, save the soft plodding of her mule's hooves in the dust of the trail, and that was not enough. Her head bobbed drowsily. Would she ever catch up with the herd?

Suddenly, catching sight of movement off the trail on her left, Larnie was wide awake. She saw a grayish-white blur in the grass some twenty yards away. A dog? No, it wasn't a dog; the animal loping along parallel to her was larger than a dog. Its movements were too wildlike for a dog.

A shiver of fear raced along Larnie's spine when another animal, similar to the first but darker in color, appeared from nowhere to join the first. Wolves! Larnie was unable to take her eyes off them. She was sure the wolves were as long as she was tall. They were frightfully lean and so hungry-looking, and they loped patiently along beside her in the grass at the edge of the quarter-mile-wide cattle trail.

Above the hammering in her chest Larnie could hear her father's voice. She remembered that he had said, when they first bought the farm, that wolves were getting to be a big problem for Kansas farmers with stock. Since so many buffalo had been slaughtered for their hides, there was little left for wild wolves to prey on except horses and cattle. And people? Larnie wondered. Was that why the shaggy creatures hovered there, never stopping or turning aside for long? Did they want *her*, or was it Sunflower that they were after?

"Wolves like easy prey," she remembered Papa saying, "sick creatures, the old and slow, or the very young." Easy prey. Mixed feelings of guilt and horror began to grow inside Larnie. She lifted the floppy brim of her bonnet and turned for a long look over her shoulder, back across the open prairie. She hoped to see nothing. A soft cry escaped her when she noticed the small figure jogging steadily along in her trail. Buzzard.

Not that she was surprised to see him. Because she had walked much of the time, had held Sunflower to a walk due to the mule's bad leg, she worried that Buzzard might catch up to her. It was possible he had awakened and set out after her as soon as she left the Ninnescah River behind.

With reluctance, Larnie admitted to herself that Buzzard had shown kindness to Sunflower. He could have gone on, ridden the lame mule into the ground, if he had chosen. A vision of the boy asleep with his thumb in his mouth swam before her eyes. Afoot, Buzzard would be the easy prey Papa had spoken of.

Yet, Buzzard wanted her mule in the worst way! He would stop at nothing to get it. He couldn't care a whit if she never caught up to the Hunter herd, got her cow back. She would be foolish to help him.

She must, though. He was a human being. There ought to be two of them, she and Buzzard united against the wolves, should the animals attack. Larnie reined Sunflower about. A faint echo in the back of her head warned, "Skitterbrain!" Larnie closed her mind and heart to the voice and continued on toward Buzzard.

Her heart beat faster when she saw that the wolves were watching her. They stopped, then turned back with her, keeping pace off to the side. Larnie shuddered and murmured a small prayer, "Keep away. Stay over there where you are, please."

When she was close enough for him to hear, she called out softly, "Buzzard, wolves. Look." She pointed to the brutes slinking through the grass. "I think we will have a better chance together."

41

Buzzard nodded. Larnie saw that a dead jack-rabbit bobbed from his belt. If they had to, perhaps they could sacrifice the rabbit to the wolves, although she hoped they could cook and eat it themselves. She would like an end to this constant gnawing in her middle.

Larnie dismounted. "You ride a while," she told Buzzard, with a sigh. His face, under the dirt, looked pale, haggard. "You're not to try to take my mule," she added in a firm whisper. "But I will share her. We can take turns, one riding, the other walking, as long as Sunflower limps, and until we reach Jeru Hunter and his cattle herd. I don't have to do this. I probably shouldn't. I'm only slowing myself down from getting my cow. Do you understand? Will you be fair?"

Buzzard nodded mutely, too out of breath to speak aloud. His eyes told Larnie little, except that maybe he was as frightened of the wolves as she was.

"Let's not take our eyes from them for a moment," Larnie whispered. "Oh, I do wish they would just disappear!"

A long while later, Larnie broke the tense silence. "Do you think they are going to attack us?" she asked Buzzard. For the first time in perhaps a half hour she turned her glance from the loping wolves to the boy astride her mule. He looked more rested now. Color was coming back to his grubby cheeks. He shrugged. "Dunno. 'Long as we stay bunched together, you an' me an' the mule, and keep movin', maybe not."

"That's what I thought," Larnie said. After a moment she added, "It's strange. You and I aren't exactly friends, but we do need each other." His answer was a spat, the brown juice landing in the dust on the opposite side of Sunflower from where Larnie walked.

When they came to Cowskin Creek, they found it steep-banked and nearly empty. Buzzard, and Larnie leading Sunflower, waded into the sluggish brown water and halted on the far bank. "Let's build a fire, cook the rabbit, and give Sunflower a chance to graze," Larnie said wearily.

While Buzzard built the fire and cleaned the rabbit, Larnie stood in the shade of a straggly hackberry shrub with a hand above her eyes to block the dazzle of the afternoon sun so she could look for the wolves. "I don't think the wolves crossed the river," she called to Buzzard after a moment. "I can't see them anywhere. Do you think they'll be coming after us?"

Buzzard grunted. "Reckon we'll see 'em again after I've had me a good dinner. Them wolves know I ain't good eatin' with my ribs stickin' to my backbone."

Larnie smiled in spite of her fear. Her mouth

began to water as the rabbit browned and filled the air with a delicious smell.

"I still have two dried apple slices for dessert," she said hopefully, "if —"

"You kin have some of my rabbit," Buzzard growled. "You done me a good turn."

"I wonder," Larnie said later, as they ate the blackened rabbit meat while squatting by the fire, "if wolves are afraid of fire in the daytime? I still haven't seen any sign of them."

Buzzard, busy eating, didn't answer.

Larnie was hungry for talk and, still curious about the boy, she said, "Buzzard, did you run away from home? Does your family know where you are?"

For a long time Buzzard looked at his grimy feet and finally directed his answer to them. "My pa has a no 'count farm down in Injun Territory. There was him, Ma, an' eighteen of us young'uns. Half of us went hungry every meal. I wanted better, got me the notion of bein' a cowboy. After Pa — after Pa —" Larnie watched, astonished, as a look of terrible hurt came over Buzzard's face. He fell silent, and she knew she mustn't ask him any more now.

Larnie traced a finger in the dust before finally saying, "I used to live in the city — in Leavenworth, Kansas. I miss it so much, my friends and all." Her throat filled up, and it was a moment before she could go on. "You couldn't picture how wonderful it was in Leavenworth," she told Buzzard, "unless you lived there once yourself. We had three or four play parties a month. We wore our prettiest dresses, drank lemonade, ate tiny cakes." She sighed.

Buzzard did not look very interested, but once begun, Larnie couldn't stop talking. "My friends and I liked to play Old Mother Wobble Gobble. It starts with someone reciting a rhyme: 'Old Mother Wobble Gobble, pray pity you, Old Mother Wobble Gobble, do as I do.' The leader then makes a terrible face or does some other funny thing, which the others have to imi —"

"Shet up!" Buzzard cried, suddenly on his feet, stomping out the small fire. "Wobble-gobble, bobble-dobble," he mocked. "Girls talk so silly. Take another turn ridin'. I got to walk off the stomachache your prattle give me."

Larnie jumped up. She probably had sounded foolish, but maybe this stupid boy liked this hot prairie with wolves lurking about. Her mouth quivered. What did he know about a place like Leavenworth? Larnie refused to look Buzzard's way as she climbed aboard Sunflower and jiggled the reins to be off. As far as she was concerned, Buzzard-whatever-his-name-was didn't exist. She would go on for Bessie alone!

"The wolves is follerin' again," Buzzard stated

suddenly, later, jarring Larnie into realizing that the boy still walked close behind her while she rode the mule. Larnie looked and spotted the wolves loping just as before to the left of them. "Don't they ever give up?" she cried in anguish.

Ahead of them Larnie could see a gray-green stretch of prairie covered all over with strange small brown mounds of earth, and she temporarily forgot the wolves. "Look! What are they?" she said, pointing to the tiny buff-colored creatures that were staring back at them from atop many of the mounds.

"A prairie-dog town, an' a big 'un!" Buzzard chortled. "Look at that!"

"They're cute," Larnie agreed, delighted. "I think they are barking at us — listen..." The shrill barking coming from the watchful prairie dogs crouching at the entrances to their burrows did sound very much like the barking of dogs. Larnie laughed.

The wolves, whom they had forgotten about, were suddenly there. Larnie watched, frozen, as they lunged every which way in violent motion through the prairie-dog town. Most of the prairie dogs had disappeared down their burrows, but some were not so fortunate, and the small screams of animal terror tore at Larnie's heart. Tears spurted from her eyes. "Get up!" she yelled at Sunflower. "Go!" She rode away fast and did not look back.

Later, Larnie let Buzzard catch up. She turned Sunflower over for his turn at riding. Walking alongside, she swallowed against the lump in her throat and asked, "Do you think, now that the wolves aren't so hungry, that they will still follow us?"

Buzzard shrugged noncommittally. Finally he said, "Poor little prairie dogs. But that's the way of it. Every creature's got to eat, an' we can thank them little buggers."

They did not see the wolves again. It was late in the afternoon when Buzzard asked Larnie how long she had been away from home. Larnie looked at the sky. "Two days," she answered through a dry throat, hardly able to believe it was true.

"You ought to go back," Buzzard grunted. "You ain't got nothin' left to eat, ain't no sign of that herd now. Looks like you ain't goin' to catch up with it. Why don't you go on back home?"

Larnie's answer came from the very depths of her being. "I would like to do that more than anything else in the world. But I can't. Not without my cow." She shook her head and her eyes grew blurry. "I thought my papa would catch up with me, help me get Bessie. Something must have happened to keep him from coming to look for me.

Or," she sighed, "he is leaving it to me to find Bessie by myself. That's been Papa's way, ever since we bought our farm."

Buzzard threw Larnie a superior look. "Well, sure. A man's got a man's work to do. He can't go botherin' hisself about a milk cow. Milk cows is women's worry. Meat critters is men's work."

Larnie looked to see if Buzzard actually meant the foolish thing he had just said. When she saw that he did, she could hardly bring herself to reply. But in a moment she said generously, "I do hope you get to be a cowboy. About Bessie, you don't understand, I guess. She isn't simply a cow. Bessie is the only thing that can keep my mama's baby alive, once it is born. If that isn't important, I don't know what is!" Beginning to feel really angry now, Larnie asked, "Why do you think I am here? Miles from anyplace, starved enough to eat my own arm, scared sick of wolves, and — and you, and everything?!"

Buzzard looked at Larnie in surprise, a weak smile playing around his tobacco-stained mouth. "So maybe you got a little grit in you, for a girl," he said. "Or maybe you're just stupid."

Larnie halted in her tracks. "That does it! Give me my mule, right now. I'm riding!" Her chest heaved with indignation. Buzzard grinned slightly as he turned Sunflower over to her, but Larnie detected reluctance in his movements. Was he still planning to steal her mule?

For the next few hours they did not speak. When the haystack appeared ahead and eastward of them, pink and mauve ribbons of sunset streaked the sky in the west.

"Somebody's cut and dried wild prairie hay," Larnie heard Buzzard say from behind her. "Jeru Hunter musta had a time keeping his herd out of it. Farmer's home place is yonder, likely. I reckon I'll stay the night in that haystack."

Larnie's eyes ached to see some other sign of civilization, but there was none. "I will, too, I suppose," she said unhappily, turning Sunflower off toward the haystack. In a short while they reached it. Larnie watched Buzzard make himself a nest in the fragrant golden needles, then she urged Sunflower around to the other side. "What if there are snakes in this hay?" she called to Buzzard as she dismounted.

There was a moment of silence; then Buzzard grunted, "Jest tell 'em to move over."

Larnie glared in Buzzard's direction, carefully examined the hay for herself in the half-light and, feeling uneasy, made ready to spend the night. There was nothing to hobble her mule with, no tree to tie her to. Larnie's shoulders slumped, then straightened. She tied Sunflower's reins about her wrist and lay thankfully back in the hay. After coming this far, she told herself, she was picking up some grit, and not all on the outside. If Buzzard tried to take this mule from her during the night, she'd fight.

In spite of her tiredness, Larnie could not fall asleep. She lay listening to the night sounds: the cooing of turtledoves, the faraway yelp and howl of a coyote or wolf, the close-by rustlings in the haystack.

Sleep came at last. In a beautiful, vivid dream, strong arms lifted Larnie and carried her to her own soft bed. "Thank you, Papa," she murmered as he tucked her in. She smiled happily.

Next morning, Larnie awakened slowly. Her first thought was that she had become used to the haystack to the point where it seemed actually comfortable. She stirred lazily, her eyes closed, and sniffed the delicious smell of side meat and cornmeal mush cooking. Food cooking? It wasn't a dream, then. Papa *had* brought her home in the night. But Mama shouldn't be up fixing breakfast. Larnie snuggled deeper into her quilt; in another minute she would get up.

"Lucas! John! Come eat. I'll fetch something to the little girl."

Larnie shot straight up in bed. Her eyes snapped open, her breathing nearly stopped. She did not know the voice she had just heard. Throwing aside the quilt, she scrambled from the bed to her feet, wearing only her petticoat and underdrawers, and stared, wild-eyed. She whirled in a circle, looking at the whitewashed mud walls, the greased-paper window, the crude furniture, which was like the furniture at home. But she was not home.

"Stars in Goshen!" the same voice exclaimed behind her, and then there was a loud clatter of dishes on the floor.

Larnie swung around and faced a darkly tanned little prune-faced woman in a faded blue gingham dress. She stared at Larnie as if she were a ghost. A plate of food she had been holding had crashed in a mess on the floor. "I seen all!" she cried, and clapped a wrinkled brown hand over her mouth.

"Where am I?" Larnie got out, "what's happened?" Seeing her dress on a chair by the bed, Larnie snatched it and pulled it over her head. Her heart beat in panic. She yanked hard, heard the cloth rip. She settled the dress in place, only half aware of the gaping rip at the waist.

The woman shook her head. "It's a miracle. You're on your feet, standin' up!" A smile warmed her lined face. "Why, your little brother told us the doctor said when the disease hit you, you'd be crippled for life. An' look at this!"

"I don't know what this is all about," Larnie protested, "please tell me." A warning gong was going off in the back of her mind, but it was a fuzzy, skittering thinking that Larnie could not pin down.

"Course you know," the woman laughed, with a wave of her hand. "You and your little brother, both of you orphans, were on your way to your Uncle Jeru Hunter's, in Wichita."

Larnie gaped, tried to break in, but the woman went on. "You were tryin' to get there before this rare disease hit you that your doctor's been warnin' you about. Like a bolt of lightning, 'long about sunset last evening, the pestilence struck you, your little brother told us. Poor little thing, you. He said you had no control over your legs a'tall."

Larnie stumbled to the chair and dropped into it. He had done it. Buzzard was somehow behind this awful nightmare. Why? To take off with her mule! "Where is my little brother?" she asked, her face hot, as anger began to replace her earlier shock.

"Stars in Goshen, the boy was off by first light this morning, hardly give me time to fix him a decent breakfast. He said he'd find your Uncle Jeru and come back with a wagon to get you. I told the little feller he'd best bring the Wichita doc back with him, too. But, look now." She pointed as Larnie stood up and walked toward her.

"I think I know what—" Larnie began, but the woman interrupted, taking her hand.

"You come on out here to the table, so I can show my boys." She led Larnie into a large main room. Two blond young giants, wearing the rough patched garb of prairie farmers, sat at a table in the center of the room. They looked at Larnie in surprise. "Luke, John, would you look? Little girl ain't crippled a'tall this morning."

"I can explain," Larnie tried again. "I'm not crippled, I never was. The boy who told you that just did it to steal my mule."

The men, one hardly more than a boy and handsome, the other lantern-jawed and serious, still looked puzzled. But they began to mouth their food again as fast as their forks could lift. The older brother gestured for Larnie to join them at the table. "We're the Hillyers — Ma, Luke, and me. Welcome."

She went, hesitated by an empty chair, then quickly sat down. "My name is Larned. Larned Moran. I live southwest of here with my papa and mama on a farm." Larnie closed her eyes, feeling dizzy, then she looked again at the men's plates. Fried cornmeal mush, fried sidemeat with gravy, honey, and biscuits. Chicken a lá king served on Aunt Helena's best rose china had never looked this good.

Larnie swallowed and gripped both sides of her chair. A few dried apples and some burned rabbit had not been enough to keep her satisfied for two days. "I went to look for our cow, Bessie...." she started again.

"Wait." The little prune-faced woman, who'd been cleaning up the spilled plate, joined them at the table. "I'll fix you some victuals, little lady. We can talk after something has been done about your empty stomach. I heard it fussin' when we were yonder."

Larnie's face pinked, and she placed a hand over her noisy stomach. Her glance fastened on the woman filling the plate, and her hand trembled as she reached for it. Never before in her life had she been so aware of the marvelous textures and flavors of food. She closed her eyes and chewed religiously, gradually easing the aching abyss that was her stomach.

Abruptly, it came to Larnie that Ma Hillyer was still talking. "My John found you. Your mule had come snuffling around our door. When John went to catch it, the mule ran from him to the haystack, where he found you, asleep. Your little brother woke up just as John come. Right off he told John you were lame and begged him not to wake you."

Somehow Sunflower's reins had come loose

from her wrist, maybe she had picked them loose in her sleep, and it had resulted in all this, Larnie thought. That Buzzard! He had had the nerve to get a good night's sleep in a bed before taking off with her mule, after telling his whopping lie. No doubt he had lost some of that nerve before he'd had a chance to eat a really good breakfast. He deserved to be hungry!

When she had finished her own meal, Larnie told the Hillyers the truth — about following the herd to recover her cow Bessie, about Buzzard and how she met him.

The Hillyers listened, concern, amusement, and shock taking turns in their expressions. "The scamp," Ma Hillyer kept saying, "the little scamp!"

"We reached your haystack last night," Larnie finished. "I was asleep when you carried me to the house, but I sort of remember thinking it was my papa, carrying me home," she told John.

John looked at Larnie thoughtfully a moment. "I've heard tell of settlers' milk cows being took into wild beef herds by mistake," he said, stroking his long jaw. "Those folks figured they had no choice but to go without milk. Hope that someday they could buy another cow — it bein' next to impossible to find their cow in a herd of thousands."

Larnie nodded, gnawing at her lip. "I know. But I have to have my cow because —" She stopped short of explaining why Bessie was sorely needed, a glimmer of an idea in the back of her mind. These folks were farmers, maybe they had a milk cow! The Hillyers were kind folk, anyone could see that. When she told them about the baby, surely they would be glad to lend them their cow, or let Papa buy it. She wouldn't have to go one step farther, she could start home this very morning!

She asked breathlessly, looking from one Hillyer to another, "Do you have a milk cow?"

The Woman in Black

Larnie might have mentioned the moon, from the smile that came to Ma Hillyer's wizened face. "Law, no, we ain't got a milk cow, much as I'd like to have one. Oh, my! Milk, cream, butter — they're so good for fixin' victuals the way they ought to be fixed."

"We got a pair of oxen we brought from Missouri, for plowin'," the younger son, Lucas, put in. "We got horses for gettin' where we got to go. A milk cow ain't as necessary."

In a quiet voice, Larnie explained why a milk cow was necessary at her home.

Ma Hillyer rocked back in her chair, shaking her gray head. "I wish I was neighbor to your mama. We womenfolk need each other so in times like this. But the prairie is big. We're scattered miles and miles apart." Her eyes sparkled with tears. "You do got to have a milk cow, honey, I know about this kind of thing. A young teacher back home lost her babe to starvation because she had no milk for it."

Something tightened in Larnie's chest, then she saw Ma Hillyer's face brighten. "We'll lend you a horse," the woman announced, "you can get to that herd faster, get your cow. The trail is straight west of here, a mile."

"She'd best give up and go on home," the older son, John, persisted. "The prairie ain't no place for a little girl alone. Someday this'll all be peaceful farm country, but that ain't the way of it now."

His mother waved him to be silent. "Pay no mind to John," she said. "Go on after your cow, honey. Wouldn't be the first time one of us womenfolk did a thing that couldn't be done. The little bay, Kate," she told her sons, "saddle Kate. On her way home Larnie can leave Kate off to us."

Aglow with gratitude, Larnie found it hard to speak. "Thank you," she said finally, with a direct look into Ma Hillyer's eyes. "I'm going to tell my mama and papa how good you have been to me, when I see them. Thank you for the horse, the bed, breakfast. I was nearly starved. I ate too much. I'm sorry."

"Hush." Ma Hillyer laughed. "Got plenty. We don't know no strangers. Ain't many that comes to our door, but those that do are friends. Don't recollect a young girl ever comin' by, though, 'crippled' or otherwise." She looked worried. "What I'd like to do is send my boys to do your errand for you. But some eastern fellers are comin' for Luke and John to take on a two, three-day buffalo hunt. Now that buffalo are gettin' fewer, easterners don't come to hunt often. When they do, it is the only cash money we get in maybe a year's time."

Larnie drew her shoulders up. "It's all right." She pulled on her bonnet and tied it under her chin. "I've come this far. The loan of your horse will make things easier from now on."

"That worthless little scamp can't be too far ahead of you, on your mule." Ma Hillyer said with a confidential smile, "You won't have any trouble catchin' up to him on Kate. You give the rascal a thumpin' for tricking us, will you?"

Larnie smiled. "I'll be happy to."

Outside, Luke was throwing a saddle on a sturdy reddish-brown mare. While Larnie waited, she looked around and saw that the Hillyers' sod shanty, with its shored-up dirt walls and weeds blooming on the sagging roof, was much like their own sod house. A walled-in well and a washtub on a platform centered the hard-packed dirt yard. There was a scraggly cornfield behind the house, and beyond that Larnie could see two more horses grazing.

A movement caught from the corner of her eye

brought Larnie's attention back to Luke, who was waving her toward the mare. Larnie stepped forward; she stroked the mare's beautiful long face for a moment. "We'll get along fine, won't we, Kate?" she said softly. The mare's ears twitched.

Luke helped her mount. John, standing aside, grunted, "I still say you ought to go on back home. Ain't nothin' hardly so stubborn as a woman, even a half-pint woman," he said, grinning slightly. "So go on after your cow. I hope you get her. Be careful, though."

Ma Hillyer said nothing, but she looked up at Larnie and reached out to pat the girl's knee. Tears welled up in the little woman's eyes and she scurried back into the sod shack.

Larnie's chin trembled. "Tell her good-bye for me. Thank you again. Good-bye." She waved.

It wasn't long before Larnie once again rode north on the hoof-torn cattle trail. She found riding in the comfortable saddle on the swift-paced mare a dream compared to jolting along on her barebacked mule. That was Buzzard's lot, for the time being. She should catch up to him soon. What a surprise she would be to the good-for-nothing windy-tongue!

Larnie began to hum a tune, then sang a few of the words as she cantered along:

"Oh, dear! What can the matter be?

Dear, dear, what can the matter be?
Oh, dear! What can the matter be?
John-ny's so long at the fair.

He promised to buy me a trinket to
*   please me,*
And then for a kiss, O he vowed he
*   would tease me,*
He promised to bring me a bunch of blue
*   ribbons*
To tie up my bonnie brown hair."

What a splendid blue-sky morning! What a difference a good night's sleep, good food, and a fine horse made. There was more food, too, in the salt sack tied to the saddle horn — corn cakes sandwiched with honey, crisp cooked meat. When she caught up with Buzzard she would dangle her treasure under his ornery nose.

Thinking of the Hillyers' hospitality, Larnie wished she had had time for a bath, time to wash her dress and mend it. But there was no time to spare.

Some time passed before Larnie spotted the small moving object far ahead. "My," she whispered to herself, "if it isn't my little brother." She clicked her tongue and nudged the bay into a fast trot. "Let's hurry, Kate. I want to talk to my little brother."

The prairie seemed to melt under the mare's flying hooves. The dark object grew in size and became a boy astride a mule. Larnie's heartbeat quickened, matching the rhythm of Kate's hoofbeats. As she watched, Buzzard turned and saw her coming. He looked back repeatedly in the next ten minutes, as though trying to decide what to do, then he halted Sunflower and waited.

"You stole yourself a horse, huh?" he commented as Larnie rode up beside him and drew Kate down to a walk. "Smart. For a girl."

"I didn't steal this horse," Larnie said, with a shake of her head. "She was loaned to me by a very nice settler woman and her sons, the Hillyers. Maybe you met them? Since a miracle cured my "crippled legs," those nice folks wanted to help me catch up with my little brother, so I could sort of look out for the—little sneak. Until we get to our Uncle' Jeru's."

Buzzard was fighting a grin. He looked straight ahead.

"That was the most unbelievable, most ridiculous, silliest lie you told, saying I was lame," Larnie told him, her face heating up. "You should have known you couldn't get by with it."

"Huh. Huh huh huh," Buzzard laughed. "I thought it was kinda' funny."

"Funny! Why, you — you — !" Larnie stormed, struggling for words. Suddenly, something inside her flipflopped, her anger switched to a giddy feeling. Her first soft chuckle surprised Larnie. In seconds she was laughing so hard that she had to grip the saddle horn to stay on the horse. She looked at Buzzard, tears streaming from her eyes. His head was thrown back and he was sending great roars of laughter into the sky.

"Goodness," Larnie moaned, "oh, my." She clutched her stomach. "I know perfectly well that I can't trust you, Buzzard, not the least bit. But I — I do sort of like you, anyway."

Buzzard darted a look at her, a faint grin of pleased surprise on his face.

A moment later, Larnie made a decision. "You can't have Sunflower for keeps, Buzzard," she told him, "but I am going to allow you to ride her until we catch up with Jeru Hunter's herd. We might have to follow all the way into Wichita, try to catch them before they ship the cows. My mama says Wichita is a wild and woolly town, a place of wicked people. I would like to believe you will stay by me, help me, at least until I find my Bessie. In exchange for that I am willing to loan you my papa's mule, for a while."

Buzzard nodded. As they jogged on, he mumbled something about being out of chewing tobacco, and Larnie was secretly glad. Finally, Buzzard said gruffly, "You know you ain't never told me your name?"

Larnie smiled. "Sorry. It is Larnie. Larned Moran. According to Mama, I was born at Larned, Kansas, in 1864, on the Santa Fe Trail. That's Pawnee County." She sighed. "Another miserable bit of nowhere, I suppose. Papa was with the Army at Fort Larned, then. Mama says Larned has such a lovely sound. Most of the time, thank petunias, they call me Larnie, plain and simple."

"Your name's all right," Buzzard said. He unbuttoned the first two buttons of his shirt and fanned himself with a grubby hand.

Larnie tugged at the neckline of her dress, but it was useless. She was as bound up in clothing as a turkey trussed for the table. She wiped the sweat from her face on her sleeve and in a quieter tone told Buzzard about her family. "There used to be more of us Morans. Five in all. Mama told me that when I was born, I already had a brother and sister. They died of typhus that first year after Papa got out of the Army, just after he'd started homesteading. Papa gave up his big dream of farming, that time, and took Mama and me, their little baby that was left, to Leavenworth to live with Aunt Helena. I don't remember Fort Larned, of course, or our first farm. For most of my life we lived in Leavenworth."

A strange yearning swept over Larnie, and Buzzard's presence was all but forgotten. "I wish

I had known my brother and sister," she said. "I wish they had lived. Poor Mama and Papa. It must have hurt Papa bad, their dying, for it to take eleven years for him to try homesteading again."

"There's the other baby, the one your ma's about to get," Buzzard contributed, reminding Larnie that she was not alone.

"Yes, there is the new baby coming," she answered, swallowing. "I will be so wonderful, too, if only — " Larnie frowned. "I wonder where the herd is now, with Bessie?"

"Up ahead. Somewhere," Buzzard said.

A long period of silence followed, broken only by the occasional whir of a prairie chicken flying up at the side of the trail. When Buzzard complained that he was so hungry he "was plumb gut-shrunk," Larnie revealed the contents of her salt sack and they ate. The midday sun poured down on them from an immense cobalt-blue sky and they continued on in drowsy silence.

"Where'd he come from so sudden?" Buzzard asked abruptly, startling Larnie from her reverie. Larnie looked at the horseman riding hard toward them from the east and realized that she had for a full minute been listening, but paying no mind to, the sound of thudding hooves. It wouldn't be Papa, coming from the east.

Larnie at once noted the flowing hair and black

clothing whipping in the wind. "It's a woman," she whispered, "not a man." An unreal phantom horsewoman rising out of the midday heat waves? The dust swirling about the rider was real enough. For some unknown reason, Larnie's hands on Kate's reins grew clammy.

"Lady looks like a ghost, but she is real," Buzzard muttered as the wild rider waved at them. "She wants us to wait for her, but I ain't."

"No, let's not," Larnie agreed. She snapped the reins and the mare bolted a few steps, then stumbled, almost going down as its right foreleg tripped in a gopher hole that Larnie saw too late. Larnie fought to keep her seat in the saddle, watching horrified as the woman on horseback barreled at them in a swirl of dust and sand. With one arm Larnie covered her face and with her other hand gripped the reins and struggled to control the frightened mare. She knew then, with helpless clarity, that the black horse would crash into her and Kate.

When it didn't happen, Larnie waved away the dust, coughing. She gave a start when she saw the woman's hand clasping Kate's bridle. "Buzzard, help me," Larnie cried out. She looked and saw him pounding away on Sunflower, heading north. "He-el-lp," she cried again. "Buzzard, please!"

"Come, come," the woman crooned as she

might to a baby. "Now come with me." Larnie gripped the reins in an attempt to pull her horse away, but the woman's free hand landed on Larnie's in a stinging slap. In the next instant, Larnie felt the reins torn from her fingers. This couldn't be happening!

"Buzzard!" she yelped again. Larnie's call for help was drowned in the woman's high cackling laugh. For the first time, Larnie looked directly at her assailant and her throat dried.

The faded brown eyes in the lined face looked fiery one instant, vacant the next. The tangled, graying black hair was a shroud over the woman's shoulders, seeming almost a part of her soiled black dress. She rode bareback, her naked, dirt-encrusted feet hanging down on either side of the black horse.

Larnie choked back a sob that welled in her throat. She stretched forward on her horse and tried to grab the mare's rein from the woman's clawlike hand. "Please. Please let me go."

The woman cackled again. Her black horse shied and danced. "I want you to come home with me, Virginia," she crowed. "You be a good little girl."

"No! I can't. I must go on after my cow Bessie. There isn't time. Please don't stop me. I'm not Virginia. I can't come with you. Please — !" Larnie's eyes went wide as the woman turned the black horse and brought it alongside Kate. In a deft move, the woman switched the reins to the other hand and caught Larnie's waist in an iron grip. "No, oh, no," Larnie moaned, struggling as the woman dragged her from Kate's saddle onto the black horse.

The woman cradled Larnie in front of her on her horse like a baby; her arms were as strong as a man's. Larnie tried to twist free. The woman clicked her tongue close to Larnie's ear and the black horse broke into a trot. Kate obediently followed.

"Let me go back to my horse, please," Larnie begged. "Let me go. I must catch up with a herd of cattle that went by here." Her voice broke on a sob. "You're making a mistake. I'm not Virginia. I'm Larned Louella Moran. My mama and papa have a farm southwest of here, down close to Indian Territory. I am Larnie. I'm not Virginia."

What could she do? Larnie wondered in panic. This woman was mad — or nearly so. How could she get away from her? She didn't blame Buzzard for running away without helping her. How she would like to be where he was now! Larnie dried her cheeks with a gritty sleeve and tried to think.

If she went along with the woman and didn't fight her, maybe she could talk to her — make her understand that she must let her go. Larnie shook her head wearily, feeling only a glimmer of hope.

Her struggling ceased and in the woman's tight arms she became like a soft, empty bundle of rags.

Larnie began to hiccup from her dry sobs and in her ear the woman crooned, "We're almost home, Virginia, almost home." Though she couldn't see the woman's face, Larnie could tell she was smiling from the sound of her voice.

After riding for perhaps a half hour, they came suddenly upon a crude dugout carved into the side of a low, grass-covered swell in the land. There were no windows, Larnie saw as they rode up to the dugout; the door was a buffalo hide hung at the only opening. "Whoa," the wild woman said in a hoarse voice. The black horse stopped. The woman started to dismount and Larnie steeled herself as she was dragged to the ground at the same time.

"I'm not Virginia," Larnie tried again in a faint voice. The woman pulled her into the cool, shadowy dugout. "I'm not your Virginia. Please try to understand."

The woman did not release Larnie's arm as she moved about inside the darkened room. She stopped suddenly and in a moment the dugout was filled with light. Shivering, Larnie saw that the woman held a crude bowl filled with oily sand in her other hand. A wick-bound stick, upright in the sand, burned bright. They had such a lamp at the farm; Mama called it an "old hussy." Larnie clenched her chattering teeth. She could feel the warmth as the woman held the lamp near her cheek.

After what seemed the passing of an eternity to Larnie, the woman spoke.

"You — you're not — not Virginia." There was an aching disappointment in her voice, but her eyes were clear and knowing. "Virginia's been gone — gone — " she sighed. "They've all been gone so long — so long. Nobody but me. For years." Her hand dropped from Larnie's arm. She placed the lamp on the roughhewn table and sagged onto a wooden box.

Larnie could have cried out in relief, she was so glad the woman knew at last that she was not the Virginia she was looking for. Larnie resisted the urge to bolt, feeling sure the woman would instantly grab her if she tried. She rubbed her arm where the circulation had been cut off. She would be patient, Larnie decided, swallowing, but only as long as she needed to be. Even now, the herd could be nearing Wichita, soon to be loaded on the cars of a freight train.

Cautiously, Larnie moved to sit on a box on the other side of the table. She would talk as she had planned. With effort, she managed to look squarely into the troubled eyes across from her. "You say you live here all alone? How do you manage? I didn't see crops, or stock, just your horse."

The eyes looking back at Larnie seemed to be struggling with thought. They went vacant an instant, then cleared again, knowing. "Buffalo," the woman in black answered. She rubbed a hand down over her bronze face. "My horse and I are great hunters — great hunters. Wild greens, berries, in the summertime." Childlike, she asked Larnie, "What do you eat?"

Larnie attempted a smile. "When I'm home, the same. Meat, corncakes, green things from our garden."

"You're pretty," the woman said admiringly, in a quick change of subject. "I don't see pretty folks, any folks, sometimes...sometimes..." Losing her train of thought, her voice trailed off. Finally, she went on, "...for...for a whole year. They run from me. I want to see folks, I want to talk. But there is nobody, nobody." The woman smothered a sudden cackle with her hand. "I talk to my horse, Midnight," she confessed.

Larnie shrugged. "I talk to myself, sometimes." She smiled, realizing she no longer had to pretend interest in this poor, lonely woman. "Where is your family?"

A long silence followed. Larnie was shocked to see tears well up in the vacant eyes. The thin lips quivered, then the woman said, "Fire. Fire came rolling across the prairie that day. Smoke. High, high, red flames. It came — burning — our barn, our house, my husband, Sam, trying to save our critters. My little Virginia... I lost her. I couldn't see. Smoke... flames... everywhere."

Slowly, Larnie's fingers reached out to touch the woman's hand, which lay on the table. "I'm — I'm sorry," she choked, "so sorry. What — how did *you* get away from the fire?"

"Climbed down into our well. Waited," the woman said.

For a moment Larnie couldn't speak, then she whispered, half to herself, "I — I was down in a well once, not long ago. Somehow — somehow, I didn't think — but it would be a safe place, from fire."

"I came out of the well," the woman went on, "it was black, after the prairie fire. Darkness. Darkness like the bottom of a bucket of pitch. No house, no barn. No sheds, no fences. I couldn't even see where they had been. My throat was full of ashes. I could barely breathe. They were gone. I was alone. All alone in cinders and blackness. Alone."

Larnie closed her eyes and fought the sobs threatening in her throat. She squeezed the warm hand inside her own, almost wishing she were Virginia. She did wish she could somehow bring happiness into the life of this poor soul. But she

was Larnie Moran, not Virginia. And Larned
Moran had to find Bessie for a little unborn baby.

After a time, when she could speak, Larnie told
the woman, "I have to go, you know." The woman
didn't reply. Larnie waited another moment. She
stood up, started for the buffalo-skin door. "I
must go," she said again.

Outside, astride the bay mare, Larnie heard a
voice inside the dugout say, "Good-bye, Virginia."

Have You Seen Bessie?

Larnie picked up the reins and pressed her knees firmly against Kate's sides. As they bolted away she looked back at the dismal dugout through a film of tears. No wonder the poor woman's mind was nearly gone. The fire and living alone in a hole in the ground would do that.

John Hillyer had said, and Papa had often remarked, that this prairie would one day be dotted with farms. When? In time for the woman in black to have neighbors? How nice it would be, Larnie thought, if the poor woman had kin who would come and take her away to the city, where there were lots of folks to visit, where life was easier.

Larnie sighed and shook her head. Papa ought to see that poor woman, if he thought living out here on the prairie was so fine. Thinking of Papa reminded Larnie she was still far from her goal: claiming her brindled cow and bringing her home.

Keeping the mare to a fast trot, Larnie came to

the trail and swung north. Although it was almost too strange to believe, two and a half days had passed since she had first learned that Bessie was missing and Buzzard had stolen Sunflower the first time. A second thing that was hard for her to understand was that Papa hadn't come to help her in all that time. She could envision Papa, though, telling her, "If you just won't be a scary chicken running for cover at every little thing that happens to you, you can get Bessie by yourself. Courage isn't something you're born with. You learn it. You learn it by facing head-on whatever it is that has you quivering in your boots. Go on now..."

"I'm going, Papa," Larnie whispered aloud. "I am. But Buzzard's gone on to Wichita without me, and he's got our mule. I'm not going to bother myself about that, though. It seems to me that the important thing is for me to get Bessie, for the baby."

Some time later, Larnie noted a blot on the horizon northwest of the trail. She leaned forward in the saddle and shaded her eyes for a better look. It was a dust cloud, no doubt about that, but if it was the cattle herd, Mr. Jeru Hunter had changed direction a bit. It didn't look far off, though. Surely she could catch up.

"This way, Kate," Larnie said gleefully, tugging at the rein and pointing the mare's head toward the blot of dust hanging above the horizon. "It won't be long now." She urged the horse into a gallop. "Good girl," she panted. The wind whipped her face, stung her eyes and caused them to blur. "Before you know it, we'll have Bessie, and you can go home."

Larnie came closer. The individual animals in the herd took identifiable shape. Buffalo! She drew the mare to a halt, then guided the horse back to the trail, close to tears in her disappointment. "Why couldn't it have been the cattle herd?" Larnie whimpered. "Why couldn't it have been?" The buffalo must have been running from the west before she saw them, raising the dust, but they were grazing now. When Larnie looked again, the shaggy beasts were moving her way. Her heart climbed into her throat.

The buffalo stayed in view the rest of the afternoon but were never close. Larnie rode on in the lonely silence of her weary self, her chin bobbing from time to time on her chest, her eyes closed more often than not, her body aching from the long day on horseback.

As though in a dream, she looked up much later and saw low lumps etched against the skyline, lumps that looked like buildings, like the buildings of a town. Larnie rubbed her eyes and looked more carefully. Yes! There was a windmill tower, another, and there — another. A smattering of trees, here and there. Then squatty houses and taller buildings came into view. A town. Wichita. The thudding of Larnie's heart seemed to fill the prairie with sound. She gave Kate a pat. "Look there," she said, "let's hurry."

Larnie's stiff, aching body tingled now with nervousness. Bessie was ahead, close...providing the Hunter herd had not been shipped out already to the Chicago packing plants....

It seemed to Larnie that there was something close to the ground, slightly moving masses of something, between her and the town, but she could not make out what it was, for sure. She held her breath, hoping, and rode on.

It was Mr. Hunter's cattle, and her Bessie. Oh, wonderful dream come true, Larnie thought, with a tired laugh. She straightened in the saddle. "Kate, we've done it," she said joyfully. "We are here. We won't have to go into Wichita. Oh, Mama would be happy about that, if she knew."

Mama had been to Wichita with Papa just once, but her opinion of the prairie cow town had never changed. "Awful," she had said, frowning and shaking her head, "just terrible. Dirty. Wild. Full of the wickedest folk on God's precious earth."

Feelings of relief and gratitude that her long trek was near an end made the final distance between Larnie and the cattle close quickly. She noted three cowboys riding at a walk around the fringes of the huge herd, and as she came near Larnie could hear one of them singing in the twilight. She relaxed further as her ears caught the slow, gentle words:

"Oh, slow up, dogies, quit roaming around;
You have wandered and trampled all over the
ground.
Oh, graze along, dogies, and move kind of
slow,
And don't be always on the go.
Move slow, little dogies, move slow.
Hi-yo, hi-yo, hi-yo."

With a deep sigh, Larnie pointed Kate toward one of the riders. Courage, Larned Louella Moran, she told herself silently, her lower lip clenched between her teeth.

She saw through the dusky evening that the rider was an older man, sunk deep in the saddle, grizzled and gray. Larnie swallowed drily as she approached him. She looked cautiously up into the eyes turned on her and was glad to see they were quiet eyes, if not outright friendly.

"I'm here for my cow Bessie," she said with a gulp, wasting no time getting to the point of her mission. "Bessie is a brindle milk cow with a black crescent moon on her shoulder." Larnie waited. The old cowboy stared at her, saying nothing, so she went on. "The foolish thing got away from where I had her tethered on our farm, by the creek. She ran away, mixing herself right into your herd when it passed our farm — about thirty or forty miles south of here. Will you please cut her out of your herd for me?"

The old cowboy knuckled his hat back and scratched his forehead.

"Mebbe I'm dreamin' or then again mebbe I'm actually lookin' at a draggletail little gal on a horse come out of nowhere." He cocked his head one way, then the other, firmed his hat back down and started to ride away. "I ain't got your cow, sis."

"What do you mean?" Larnie yelled after him, her voice rising to an unnatural pitch as she fought against tears. "I've followed this herd for three days. You've got my Bessie in it! I know this herd!"

He pulled his mount to an abrupt halt. "You tryin' to tell me you seen every one of my three thousand cows before and you can recognize each and every one, even in the half dark?" The old man, looking back at her, shook his head in mock astonishment. "I sure am dreamin'. Must be somethin' Cookie is puttin' in the beans, givin' me nightmares."

It was all Larnie could do to keep from bursting into angry, wailing sobs. She set her jaw against its quivering. She would not let this be a situation to make light of, not when the life of a tiny baby lay at the heart of it. She wouldn't. "I don't know why you won't talk straight with me, but this is important. I am not lying, I'm not joking. I don't want anything that isn't mine. I'm telling you the truth. Please, are you Mr. Jeru Hunter, or is he your boss?"

The old man sobered and lifted a hand in a sign of truce. "Awright. No more funnin'. You have made a mistake, miss. Jeru Hunter got in with his herd yesterday. He's holdin' his critters yonder west. We been here more'n a week. You see, there's five big herds bein' held outside town, along the Arkansas River, waitin' fer some dickerin' fer better prices to be settled."

"Wait," Larnie pleaded. "I don't understand. Do you mean five herds, this size, are here?" She gripped the saddle horn with both hands, as though hanging on to a last thread of hope, but she knew in her heart the answer would not be what she wanted to hear.

"Yup. More'n twenty thousand head of the old mossy-horns, all told."

As she tried to picture it, Larnie's mind protested. It can't be! "Twenty thousand? But — but —" Feeling faint, Larnie fastened her glance on Kate's heavy mane in a wide-eyed stare. She gripped the reins, trying to hold steady as she began to weave in the saddle. You could look for days in that many thousands of animals and never catch sight of the one cow you were looking for.

Larnie tried to thank the cowboy for his help, but no words would come. She reined Kate away. How long Larnie circled the mare — toward home, toward Wichita, toward home again — she didn't know. But when Larnie felt the full impact of having lost Bessie for good she halted the horse. "Poor little baby," she choked out. "Poor little thing. I have to keep trying."

The old cowhand, evidently hearing, rode alongside Larnie. "That Jeru Hunter can be pesky to deal with. Man's got a bad leg, some kind of open sore that keeps comin' back on him from an old wound he got in the war — makes him touchy as a teased snake most of the time."

Larnie looked at the cowboy without really seeing him. For three days she had tackled more than she would ever have dreamed she could. It might be that she could find Bessie among twenty thousand or more cows, too. She wouldn't know until she tried. There was time to look, if what the old cowboy said was true, that the trail bosses were waiting for business deals to be made. "I'm going to find Jeru Hunter," she told the old rider; "he will just have to listen to me."

Clicking her tongue, Larnie faced the mare into the sunset and rode in the direction of Jeru Hunter's herd. In the near darkness behind her the cowboy cautioned, "You'd best go on home, gal, git your Pa to git your cow for you."

"Can't." Larnie shook her head. "No time for that."

In the descending dusk Larnie could see that long-horned cattle flecked the flat land for miles, and she knew that in her lifetime she would never again see so many cows at one time. Some of the cows closest to her were lying down, chewing their cuds, while others milled about, bawling. Larnie eyed the horns that in many instances were longer than the rockers on Mama's chair and she rode in a wide arc around the brutes.

She wished she had asked Buzzard or the old cowboy to describe Jeru Hunter for her so she would know him when she saw him. All she had to go on was that he had a bad leg, which made him ornery. No matter, she would know her cow if and when she ever laid eyes on Bessie!

Larnie didn't dare ride too close to the bedded cattle. She had read, and had often heard, that these wild cattle would stampede at almost nothing. She could be killed.

An hour passed and it was full dark. The glow of a fire, the smell of boiling coffee, and the sound of soft voices told Larnie that she had at least reached a cowboy camp. She rode in, voiced her mission. The riders squatting around the fire stared at Larnie as though they didn't quite believe what they were seeing, but they told her the Hunter camp, and holding ground, was farther west.

A soft night breeze cooled Larnie for the first time that day. Stars blinked bright above her. She weaved in the saddle, dead tired, but straightened instantly when her eyes caught sight of a second fire ahead. Setting her jaw, Larnie rode directly to the circle of perhaps a half dozen men around the campfire. She had found the right cow camp, she guessed, because in the light of the fire, with his back toward her, Larnie saw a short, bedraggled boy: Buzzard. He talked earnestly to a cowboy filling his coffee cup from a pot he lifted from the fire. Sunflower, ground-reined nearby, dozed on her feet.

Larnie relaxed. It was too dark to try to locate Bessie now, but at least she was here. She guided Kate closer to the fire. Someone voiced an exclamation. Buzzard saw her and visibly jumped. From the look of surprise on his face, Buzzard had been convinced that the woman in black had eaten her alive, Larnie decided. "I want to talk with the man in charge," she said. The strain of the days just past, and her awful weariness, made Larnie's request a croaking yelp. More heads turned.

"Another button, a girl this time," someone said in surprise. "The little sage hen looks like death."

One of the cowboys laughed. "Where they comin' from? The jimson weed sproutin' 'em all of a sudden?" The others joined in the laughter, Buzzard's boy voice louder than the others.

Larnie didn't laugh. "Which one of you is Mr. Jeru Hunter, please?"

A man close to the fire, wearing an apron, his red-brown face contrasting sharply with the whiteness of his upper forehead and balding scalp, told her, "Over yonder. The boss. Jeru Hunter."

Larnie flashed the man, who, she decided, must be the cook, a nervous smile of thanks. She lifted her chin and rode around the fire toward a lone man sitting in the shadows, a lighted lantern on his other side. He sat propped against a saddle, a book in his hand. If he was going over the count of his cows, Jeru Hunter must know he had an extra, her Bessie.

"Hello," Larnie stammered, swallowing against the dryness of her throat. While waiting for the man to take notice of her, Larnie studied him. He was shorter than Papa. He was dressed like her father in a hickory shirt, a vest, and blue Levi's. Papa, though, Larnie thought to herself, never wore a neckerchief knotted around his neck, nor high-heeled boots, nor such a wide-brimmed hat.

Nor had Papa ever looked as though he had lived in the same clothes night and day for months! And the man smelled as bad as he looked.

Larnie wrinkled her nose, thinking that it must be a long unclean time from Texas to Kansas. Well, she wasn't exactly a daisy, either —

"You done starin' at me, smellin' me?" a voice rasped angrily.

Larnie blushed painfully and jerked her eyes away. When she looked back at the man slowly, pale-blue eyes bore into hers. "I — " Larnie tore her glance from the trail boss's eyes and for the first time saw the book in his hand up close. The title on the cover surprised her: *How to Edit the Small-town Newspaper*. Would this cowboy rather be a newspaperman? Maybe, because of his leg...

"I thought you were counting up your cows," Larnie told him, looking again into the man's square, craggy face with its sandy mustache. "I thought you would know about my cow Bessie. She wandered into your herd a few days back, down near the border, just this side of Indian Territory." She leaned forward in the saddle. "I don't suppose you could look tonight, but first thing in the morning if you would cut Bessie out of the herd for me, I'd appreciate it, Mr. Hunter. You see, I have to get Bessie home before — before — "

Jeru Hunter shook his head furiously, stood up, and rubbed his leg. "Not again," he muttered. "You're about the twentieth nester kid that has made that claim this trip." His lips tightened and an angry, hard look came into his eyes. "I'd wind up with half a herd to sell if I believed all you sodbusters."

So Buzzard was right when he said some folks lied to get free cows. "I wouldn't lie, Mr. Hunter," she protested. "You've got our milk cow in your herd. I wouldn't care — I wouldn't care, not that much, really, if you kept Bessie, or if she was made into beefsteak, but — my mama —" Larnie's voice broke, and she struggled to go on, "My mama is going to have a baby — any minute, if she hasn't already. My mother was very sick all last year, she nearly died. She won't be able to feed the baby, it will starve if I don't get Bessie out of your herd and take her back home, fast."

Jeru Hunter said nothing, but the anger in his eyes seemed to lessen.

Larnie waited, determined not to back down, no matter what the man's next words might be.

"You don't want to believe a word that gal says, Mr. Hunter."

Larnie whirled in the saddle and saw that Buzzard had left the fire and stood close behind her. Larnie opened her mouth to protest, but Buzzard went on, "She been follerin' me a long time, tryin' to steal my mule by claimin' it belongs to her. You want me to run her off for you Mr. Hunter? Huh?"

"What does your cow look like?" Jeru Hunter

took in Larnie and Buzzard both in a look that was as heavy as a swiping blow.

Larnie could have cried in her relief. Buzzard was obviously trying to get on the good side of the trail boss, but Jeru Hunter must believe her!

"B-Bessie — she is a brindle — you know, black and brown streaks — "

"I've got two hundred or more brindles in that herd," Jeru Hunter snorted.

"She has golden-colored horns," Larnie went on quickly, "shorter horns than your wild Texas cows have. And there is a black crescent-moon shape on her left shoulder."

Larnie halted her tongue when the trail boss's own mouth began to spew a string of curse words that she was sure would strip the leaves from a tree, had there been a tree around. Larnie screwed up her face, blocking his words from her mind, until she heard him say, "You really think I ought to comb through over two thousand cow critters, one by one, looking for a cow with a black crescent mark on her left shoulder?"

Larnie's eyes met Hunter's in the glow from the lantern. "Yes, I do." She swallowed. "As soon as it is daylight."

All That Mama Claimed

Larnie's reply only brought another string of curse words from the trail boss. Buzzard snickered loudly and commented, "Listen to him air his lungs!"

Larnie was trying not to hear the curse words, but she understood Jeru Hunter to say he wanted only one thing: to sell this last herd and get out of the cow-driving business for good.

In that moment, a ruddy-faced, tow-headed young man of about seventeen rode into the circle of light from the campfire. He took off his hat, and his Adam's apple bobbed in his neck as he tried to speak.

"What d'you want, Hayseed?" Jeru Hunter snarled.

"I — I'm d-dead t-tired, M-Mr. Hunter," the young man stuttered. "B-bein' both day wrangler of the horses, and nighthawk, too, I ain't gettin' any sleep. C-could s-somebody s-spell me so's I can —"

"No," Jeru Hunter snapped. "I'm shorthanded now, with half the men in Wichita, tearin' up the town." He waved Hayseed off. "You can catch up on your sleep next winter."

The young cowboy looked angry, Larnie saw, and as tired as she felt, but he turned his horse and rode back into the night.

The trail boss made a limping turn and glared at Buzzard. "I'm fed up," he said, "with you, too. A button, pesterin' me for a job! Ain't nothing worse'n having a boy on a drive. Cause stampedes, all kinds of trouble." He looked at Larnie. "And I ain't got no time to worry about a blankety-blank-blank milk cow." He started off and jerked a hand for Larnie and Buzzard to follow. "The two of you come over here to the wagon. I'll have the cook get you some chuck, and find a place for you to sleep."

"Your leg botherin' you again, boss?" the bald cook asked as Jeru Hunter limped toward him. "I'll boil some water and get some towels an' fix a hot pack for it."

The trail boss grunted, "Not tonight, button kids," he growled. "Trying to turn a farmboy into a decent nighthawk. Milk cows. Sometimes," he said acidly, "I got doubts about this job." He thumbed a hand at Larnie, following him slowly on Kate, at Buzzard, walking in slumped disappointment. "Feed 'em. Find 'em a place to sleep.

After that I don't want to see a hair of either of
'em again."

Jeru Hunter returned to his saddle on the
ground, removed his boots, and rolled himself up
in a blanket. The cook motioned twice for Larnie
to dismount, but she could only stare about her in
a weary numbness. The other cowboys in camp
were now in their own bedrolls on the ground, and
one of them had already commenced to snore.
"You don't understand," Larnie babbled to the
seemingly lifeless bundles on the ground around
the fire. "Our baby...Bessie...Papa will..."

Nobody listened. After a long while, Larnie al-
lowed the cook to help her from the saddle. She
slumped down by the fire and in a wooden motion
accepted a filled plate. The sourdough bread and
hot beans tasted good. It was cozily warm by the
fire. She was so tired. Larnie's head began to nod
in spite of her efforts to hold it up. She shook
herself, took a few more mouthfuls. Later, as if in
a dream, Larnie watched the beans sliding side-
ways off her plate into her lap. Too tired to do a
thing to stop it, she watched through sagging lids
as the beans piled up in drifts in the folds of dress
in her lap.

Larnie woke up believing she could smell lilacs.
There was soft comfort under her sore body, and
above. Slowly, she opened her eyes. She lay in a

large bed in a drab yellow room. She saw a single chair by the door, frayed curtains blowing at an open window, and a bowl of faded lilacs on a table beside the bed. Larnie placed her palms flat against the mattress and sat up.

How did she get here? She remembered Jeru Hunter's cow camp. Eating by the fire... Hunter's bald cook... The cook must have brought her here to—Wichita! That's where she was, she was in a room somewhere in Wichita!

Where was Bessie? How long had she been here, sleeping? What if Jeru Hunter had sold his cows, and Bessie with them? Larnie threw back the covers and stood barefoot on the rough wooden floor. Had they brought her to Wichita to get rid of her, stop her from pestering them about Bessie? What had they done with the Hillyers' mare, Kate?

There were a pitcher of water and a washbasin on the table, besides the lilacs. Larnie washed with shaking hands, then combed her hair with her fingers and rebraided it. Someone had put her to bed fully clothed, except for her shoes, and a look down at her dirty rumpled dress brought a groan of pain and horror from Larnie. She had no other clothes, though, so there was no use to fret, she decided, putting on her shoes.

Taking a wilted lilac from the vase, Larnie fastened it to her hopeless bonnet. Carrying the bonnet by the strings, Larnie rushed to the door, then hesitated before opening it cautiously. She stepped out into a narrow, dingy hall and moved to the head of a flight of stairs. Below her was a man asleep in a chair with a newspaper, the *Wichita Eagle*, spread out in his lap.

Larnie tiptoed down the wooden stairway. She flurried across the main lobby and stopped before scarred double doors that would open, she was positive, smack into the middle of wicked Wichita. Larnie took a deep breath and reached for the doorknob.

Standing on the boardwalk outside the hotel with her legs feeling like so much cotton fluff under her long skirts, Larnie examined her surroundings. Across the way a structure designated as "Keno Hall" seemed to explode with laughter, angry shouts, and then a sudden burst of a word, "Keno!" A kind of game, Larnie decided. The shouting made her feel jumpy.

While she stood there, a lean young pig came zipping along the walk in her direction. Larnie jumped back and planted her back close to the exterior of the hotel as a plump little boy came after the pig, yelling at the top of his lungs, "Zinnia, stop, wait for me!" In the wake of the boy came a red-faced housewife, who was clutching her gingham skirts in one hand and waving a wooden spoon in the other. Larnie smothered a nervous giggle with her hand. No doubt the lady's garden was minus a few carrots or turnips this morning.

Larnie tied her bonnet in place, then pulled the floppy brim forward with the feeble hope that it would somehow hide her from the townspeople's view. She began to walk east along the street, which was lined on either side by false-fronted business houses, some built of wood and some of brick. The barnlike building ahead, marked "Livery," drew her as the most likely place to begin her search for the Hillyers' mare.

A passing bearded man jostled Larnie roughly aside. He smelled so strongly of rank animal skins that she guessed he must be a buffalo skinner, one of the worst enemies of the disappearing buffalo, according to Papa.

A yellow dog trotted by, his tongue hanging out wetly. Two ladies, with chins high and eyes unseeing, marched along on the other side of the street. Noting the pools of filth under the horses tied to the hitching racks, Larnie understood why the women walked as they did. She turned her own face away from the street, but it did not stop the vile odor from clinging to her nose, nor did it keep the droning of the flies from her ears.

As she listened to the tinny piano music and raucous laughter coming from a saloon, the creak of wagon wheels and rattle of harness out in the dirt street, the clomp of booted feet shaking the boardwalk, and the mournful wail of a train whistle in the distance, Larnie knew suddenly that she had gotten used to the peaceful quiet of their prairie farm and that at this moment she longed for it.

The train whistle! What if the money problem had been settled and the cattle herds were being shipped this morning? She must find out! At a corner a short distance farther east, Larnie came upon a horse auction being held in the street, and she heard one cowboy refer to the place, in a mumble, as "Horse Thief Corner." She would like to watch a moment, but there wasn't time.

Finally Larnie reached the livery stable. Its wide doors were open to the already hot morning sun, and there was a strong smell of horses coming from within. The clang of iron on iron sounded friendly to Larnie's ears. A rope-thin old man, who seemed to be in charge, led Larnie to the horse stalls in back. "Yes" — Larnie breathed a sigh of relief — "that's the Hillyers' mare, Kate. She is borrowed."

"Good horse," the old man stated, patting the mare's rump. "A feller I believe is Jeru Hunter's cook brought her in, paid her keep in advance, said till a little girl came for her. He tole me you'd be ridin' for home today, soon's you woke up."

Larnie shook her head, unable to hide her resentment. "I'm not going anywhere until I have my cow Bessie." She stroked Kate a moment, then asked, "Are there any cattle being shipped out today? I heard a train...."

"I don't rightly know," the hostler told her, "but it seems to me they're shippin' some all the time."

Larnie jerked about to face him. "Can you tell me, quickly, which way to the railroad where they ship the cows from?

"On east." The thin, knotty hand pointed. "Far end of Douglas Avenue, you'll find the stock-yards." A frown furrowed the man's face. "You ain't plannin' on hanging around this town long, alone, are you, sissie?"

"Just as soon as I can get our milk cow Bessie on the end of a rope, I'm heading home."

"Good idea," the old man said, his thin face serious. "Though you'll be all right, like as not, if you stay away from Delano."

"What is Delano?"

"It's a place at the west end of town, by the Douglas Avenue bridge. A lot of ornery goin's on there at night, two dance houses there, and a few shacks. More trouble'n anything, brawlin', shootin'. They keep our police busy. Wyatt Earp does a good job, though."

"I'll stay away from the place," Larnie promised. "I want to go in the other direction, now, to

the stockyards. I'm hoping my cow isn't there...
yet...."

Larnie reached the stockyards, a large network
of very odorous pens filled with bawling, shuffling
cows, by the Santa Fe Railroad. She decided
quickly that she could see best from atop the
windmill tower, and began to climb it. The wind
at the top felt cool. Larnie gripped the tower ladder and looked down at the maze of almost-new
cattle pens. Cows were in most of them. She did
not recognize Jeru Hunter, nor any of the other
cowboys she had seen in his camp, among the few
men moving about.

Then Jeru Hunter's herd was still being held
outside town! Sighing in relief, Larnie took
another minute to be cooled by the breeze and
counted: twenty-seven gates, four runways and
chutes. It would be hard to keep an eye on all the
gates, if Bessie was among the cows being
shipped. The old liveryman had said that the
stockyards could hold twenty-five hundred cows,
or one hundred carloads, at once! An average of
ten cars could be loaded in an hour. Larnie shook
her head in wonder.

As she began her descent, Larnie noted
another interesting sight along the railway. Pile
after enormous pile of buffalo and cattle bones
were bleaching to an eye-dazzling white under the
Kansas sun. It was well known that many settlers

made a living gathering these bones, which were
then shipped to carbon factories for making fer-
tilizer, and for making bone black into ink. Larnie
was glad that she and her papa and mama didn't
have to gather the smelly bones.

Larnie felt wobbly on the ground and knew it
was from more than the climb. She clutched at her
middle and it was then she felt the strange object
in her pinafore pocket. With a cautious hand she
took out a crumpled piece of paper and a hard
round coin. The note was signed by Jeru Hunter.
The scrawly writing said:

Girl. Tell your pa I will settle up with him
for the brindle milk cow. After I sell the
herd, and if I find out you are telling the
truth.

Larnie groaned and stamped her foot. Hadn't
that man listened to what she had told him?
Money for Bessie would be useless. Would money
nourish a newborn baby? Jeru Hunter's bad leg
must bother him a lot if he could think no
straighter than that. She had to have Bessie!

Larnie turned the coin over and over in her
hand. A silver dollar from Mr. Hunter. She supposed the old grouch meant it as payment to be
rid of her. Well, he wasn't. She had seen a restaurant back in the busy part of town near the Texas

House Hotel. She would eat, get Kate from the livery, and then head back for the cow camp. If they would just help her, she knew she could find Bessie.

Flies hummed in lazy circles inside the hot, airless restaurant, the place was thick with noise — the chink and clatter of dishes, the hiss of frying food, loud talk. It smelled delicious, though, and that was good enough for Larnie. She found a table facing the front window and folded her hands in front of her on the greasy red-checked tablecloth. The answer to her timid request for "ham and eggs, please" was a huge platter of food that would have fed the whole Moran family. Larnie ate it all.

She sat back in her chair and as gingerly as possible sipped the tea she'd been served with the breakfast, her greedy appetite still a blot on her conscience. As she watched, a small, red-whiskered man in an oversized gray Stetson hat and a dark, rumpled suit slipped furtively along outside the restaurant.

Larnie smiled to herself at the comic look of him. Suddenly, he returned, and this time he pressed his face to the window. His hands cupped out the bright sunlight for a better look into the dark interior of the restaurant. A chill ran down Larnie's spine, for the little man was staring long and hard at her! Or was he? Larnie's hand shook as she made a grand and time-consuming thing of adding more sugar to her tea, while pointedly ignoring the red-whiskered face at the window. When she peeked a moment or two later, the man had disappeared.

She swallowed an involuntary giggle and sagged in her chair. She sure was a scary chicken about being here in wild and woolly Wichita. Her imagination was playing molehills up into mountains.

A young girl about Larnie's own age entered the restaurant, accompanied by a taller, older version of herself, probably her mother, and Larnie quickly forgot the stranger who had been at the window. Larnie felt a sickening envy inside, and shame at her own clothes, when she noted the girl's soft-blue dress trimmed with snow-white ruffles, and the matching beribboned bonnet covering her perfect blond curls. She herself used to dress like that when they lived in Leavenworth. The pain inside her grew.

As she watched, Larnie saw the girl fuss and pout over where they should sit, in a quiet corner, as the mother wanted, or at a table in the center of the room, which the girl favored. The daughter won, but when they were seated and she argued babyishly with her mother over the food she wanted to order, the girl did not get her way. She took out a lace handkerchief and dabbed at imaginary tears, the corners of her mouth turned down in a very unflattering pout.

The sight of the empty, foolish simpering brought a bad taste to Larnie's own mouth. She paid for her breakfast and left the restaurant. Had she been like that when they lived in Leavenworth? If so, Papa was right to want her to change, to want her to grow up and stand on her own two feet. If piling work and responsibility on her shoulders was the way to help her change, she was glad!

Still, she had made an awful bobble of things. Bessie missing just when the baby was due. Having Sunflower stolen. She must get them both back, make things right again, as fast as she could. She had ceased to wonder why Papa hadn't come looking for her. She knew, with a constant uneasiness weighing in her heart, that something had taken place at home to hold Papa there. She was certain of it.

Death's Hand

Larnie started along the boardwalk toward the livery. A feeling of edginess swept over her, a feeling that she was being watched. She turned her head slowly and caught her breath. Across the street, almost out of sight in the doorway of a store, she saw the shadow of a crouching man. It was the red-whiskered man in the big hat, the one she had seen looking at her through the restaurant window!

Her feet broke into a run of their own accord. When she threw a quick look over her shoulder, she saw the man lift a cupped hand to motion her to come to him. Her throat dried, her knees threatened to buckle. She made herself run faster, eastward again on Douglas Avenue, toward the livery. She liked the old hostler there, trusted him. He would help her.

Larnie looked back a second time and saw the small red-whiskered man slipping along from doorway to doorway, after her, but still on the opposite side of the street. When he caught her looking at him, the man again motioned with a cupped hand for Larnie to hurry his way.

She would not! Larnie reached the livery stable out of breath. She ran at the old liveryman and panted, "S-saddle the b-bay for me, please." He stared down at her face, her wringing hands, his old eyes full of question. Then, shaking his head, he hustled toward the bay's stall.

"Somethin' botherin' you, sissie?" he asked over his shoulder.

"There is a man after me," Larnie babbled as the liveryman threw a saddle on Kate. "Big gray hat, dark suit, red whiskers. Will you watch, try to stop him, if he goes after me? Till I get out of town?"

"Sure I will." The old hostler nodded. "But are you sure he means harm to you, missie? Sounds like Tom McGrath. Ol' Tom is a worthless thief, a town bum, with mighty sticky fingers, but I ain't never heard tell of him hurtin' nobody."

Close to tears, Larnie shook her head. "I don't know what he wants. I just want to get out of town, now. I'm going to the holding ground, where Jeru Hunter has his cattle. He's got to give me my Bessie. I'm going home to my mama and papa!"

"Now, now," the old man soothed. "Calm down, sissie." He led Kate out into the street. "Show me this feller," he told Larnie, "the one's been followin' you."

Larnie looked, her stomach still queasy with panic. "I don't see him. He is none of those men on the street." She looked again, her glance traveling more carefully up and down both sides of the hot, dusty street, trying to see into every nook and doorway. A long-whiskered old man sat in a rocking chair on the porch of the boot shop, two riders guided their horses slowly up the street; men, women, and children were here and there on the boardwalk. Larnie shook her head. "He's gone."

"Maybe it is this heat that has got your mind playin' tricks on you," the hostler said consolingly. "I wouldn't worry. Just take care. I hope you get home with your folks soon. That's where a nice little girl like you belongs."

"Thank you. I hope I do, too." She looked at the hostler a long moment. Maybe he was right when he said she might be imagining things. This town did make her nervous. Maybe she was building up horrors in her mind out of nothing. The red-whiskered man, Tom McGrath, could have been signaling to someone else. Someone she hadn't seen. Larnie blushed, feeling silly. She mounted, waving at the hostler, and was on her way. Imagined danger or real, she was glad to be leaving Wichita and its wickedness behind.

Once she had crossed the Douglas Avenue bridge and was past the bad Delano district, she would forget Wichita and give all of her mind to the task of looking for Bessie. Kate's trotting hooves clattered as they crossed the bridge. A short while later, Larnie relaxed in the saddle, relieved to be on the hot, dusty road out of town.

There was one thing she hadn't done, Larnie thought, as Kate loped along in a soft summer wind; she hadn't ridden into the Hunter herd to look for Bessie herself. Her bottom lip caught between her teeth. The plan sent chills all through her, just thinking of it. But if she had to, she would ride into the herd. If Mr. Hunter and his cowboys didn't want to help her, they could sit by and watch!

"Hee haw, hee haw." The sudden familiar braying behind Larnie caused her to turn quickly to look. It was Sunflower, with the sorriest, saddest-looking boy astride that Larnie could ever remember seeing. She drew Kate to a walk and called back over her shoulder.

"What's wrong, Buzzard?"

His reply was scarcely audible. "They won't let me."

Larnie halted the mare. "Who won't let you what?"

"Mr. Hunter. All of 'em," he grumbled. "I wanted to go back to Texas with 'em. Help bring up the next herd. Said no. When they sell their cattle, they sell their horses, too. They go back to Texas on the train, and nobody'd buy an extra ticket for me."

"Did you tell them how bad you want to be a cowboy? Did you tell them you'd work hard?" Larnie asked.

"I told 'em! They said I'd be nothin' but trouble, a burr under a saddle blanket."

Larnie didn't dare smile at the remark, and besides, she did feel sorry for the plainly heart broken boy. "There are a lot of herds at Wichita now. Did you talk to all the trail bosses?"

Buzzard's shoulders sank impossibly lower. "Asked ever'body. Ain't nobody that wants me."

Larnie swallowed and was silent for a time, as she stroked Kate. "What will you do now? Are you going back to your family?"

Buzzard's answer seemed to be pulled from the very depths of his being and clearly caused him pain. "Pa — said — I — was — never — to — come back. Said I was to take care of me own self."

Larnie stared at him, then looked away. What kind of father would turn out a boy as young as Buzzard to make his own way? She looked back at Buzzard, who was still talking, walking Sunflower at a snail's pace.

"I been back yonder in town watchin' Professor S. Gessler, The Armless Wonder, performin'. He sure don't need arms to do nothin'. Got his feet and his teeth. I didn't see The Child Wonder and The Freak Pig; they was comin' later. Thought I would join up with them, though I ain't a freak. Wanted to play the hand organ that calls the folks with its music to come see the show. Professor Gessler didn't need me, neither. Did you see the show?" he asked Larnie.

She shook her head. "I was looking for Bessie at the stockyards. Then I ate breakfast and got Kate." Larnie sighed. "You really wouldn't want to be in a sideshow, would you, Buzzard? It's so...so...look, maybe you can't be a cowboy now, but you can when you grow up."

"Till then, what?" Buzzard muttered. "Got no place to go. Some ladies was after me in Wichita. I heard 'em sayin' that the stray kids in town ought to be rounded up and sent to Kansas City to the 'nice' orphans' home where they'd be took care of. The looks them ladies give me might as well been arrows. 'Been dodgin' 'em all mornin'. Don't want to go to no orphans' home!"

"Of course not!" Larnie agreed. "Wait," she said softly, "there was a strange man after me in town. The town bum. Do you think he may have been hired to catch kids for the orphans' home? Oooh." Larnie shook her head. "It couldn't be, could it? I do know that except for the liveryman, and maybe a few others, Wichita is all my mama claimed."

Larnie clicked her tongue and urged Kate into a lope. Buzzard, in unspoken agreement, did the same on Sunflower. Larnie threw a worried look over her shoulder. There was nothing but heat waves in the roadway.

An idea began to form in the back of Larnie's mind. "Buzzard," she said, "help me get Bessie, then come home with me. I'll need help getting her all the way home again. Come live with us on the farm!" Larnie turned in the saddle and saw a look of great joy appear on Buzzard's face, which instantly changed to one of hurt and anger.

"I can haul my own freight," he snapped. "You're pityin' me, that's all, an' it makes me sick! I don't need no help from nobody!"

"Fine!" Larnie snapped back, heat rising in her face. She held her tongue tightly between her teeth to keep from pointing out to him that he had already "taken" help from her in the form of Sunflower. She kneed the mare into a fast trot and gave Buzzard her back. Why, Larnie wondered as she rode toward Jeru Hunter's holding ground, must Buzzard be so blindly, stupidly proud!

Although Buzzard made no effort to keep up with Larnie, she knew he was following her from the steady plop, plop of Sunflower's hooves behind her. She had intended to ask where he spent the night, but now she wouldn't. Showing interest and concern in him would only cause him to yell at her, or do some other mean thing.

It crossed Larnie's mind, suddenly, that the brothers and sisters she had known in the past often acted the way she and Buzzard were behaving now. Larnie smothered a surprised giggle. She would leave Buzzard in the care of time. Once he faced the truth that he couldn't be a cowboy for a while, farming with the Moran family would seem like a good idea.

Larnie's thoughts turned ahead to her fast-approaching meeting with the trail boss, Jeru Hunter. No doubt he believed she had swallowed his refusal to help her find Bessie. He probably thought she had turned mouse-meek toward home again. How could she do that? Go home to Mama and Papa and say, "Sorry, I couldn't find the cow. Too bad about the baby. I did all I could."

There was still one thing she hadn't done. As Larnie neared the holding ground of the Hunter herd, she felt strangely cold, though the sun was hot, and she knew she would search the herd herself, if she must.

The dusty camp was quiet in the midafternoon sunshine. Three riders walked their horses at the fringes of the far-grazing herd. Closer at hand, a southwind picked at the canvas cover of the chuckwagon. Two more cowboys squatted by the tailgate of the wagon, coffee cups in hand. Jeru Hunter didn't seem to be there. He was in town, probably, Larnie decided with a lift of her nose, in one of those noisy, wicked saloons.

Larnie rode close to the cowboys by the chuckwagon, climbed stiffly down from Kate's saddle, and drew her shoulders high. She let her bonnet fall back on her shoulders, and faced the two men. "This time —" she began.

"You still aroun', little gal?" one of the riders, a Mexican, interrupted. "Don't your mama worry 'bout you, chasin' aroun' like a homeless kitten?"

Larnie believed she saw true worry in the dark eyes. Maybe this man has sisters at home, she thought. He might help her. "I know my cow Bessie is here somewhere, among these cows," she said to him. "I really have to get her out of this herd, take her home." Larnie pushed aside the damp locks of hair the wind had tossed in her face and wiped the sweat from her forehead.

Because she could no longer mention Mama and the new baby aloud without her throat filling up, Larnie did not describe her plight in detail. "I must have my cow. Will you help me look, p-please?" At the end Larnie's voice shook anyway. She took three short gulps of air.

The Mexican cowboy shrugged. "The boss —" he started to say.

The other cowboy, who had been smirking since Larnie's arrival, burst into a sudden guffaw. "Little outlaw gal," he chortled. "Cattle rustler. You got grit, trying to get yourself a cow off'n us." He got to his feet. "I got half a mind to tan your hide, teach you a lesson. Didn't your Sunday school teacher larn you that you can't steal cows?" He took a step toward Larnie, his mouth open in a wide toothless grin.

"Go home, little girl," the Mexican said softly. "Go home."

Larnie's heart beat fast. She picked up the reins, backed the bay mare from the threatening cowboy. "You won't help me, then?"

"C'mon, Reedy," the Mexican rider coaxed, faint anger in his voice. "It's time we relieved Dad and Gates."

"Shoo!" The cowboy named Reedy lunged at Larnie, roaring with laughter. "'Fore I give you the lickin' of your life!" Deep chuckles rumbled up from his chest, and he looked as though he would greatly enjoy giving her a whipping — it would probably be a happy respite for him from the dullness of his work day, like dancing or eating cake.

Larnie trembled. "Don't touch me," she warned. "Don't."

Another voice, younger, joined Reedy's in laughter. Larnie turned and saw that Buzzard had arrived on Sunflower. Buzzard was like all the rest. To most of them, her determination to get Bessie was a big joke, others simply didn't believe her, and some, like Jeru Hunter, became angry at her because she bothered them. Not one of them cared that a tiny baby might be taking its last breath this very minute. Larnie stood her ground.

"Go home," the Mexican repeated, hoisting a saddle to his shoulders. Larnie didn't bother to speak or even shake her head in reply. She waited. Reedy gave her a wave of dismissal, as if he were swatting a fly, and shouldered his own saddle. Shaking his smirking head, he followed the Mexican cowboy to the grazing remuda, the band of extra saddle horses in the keep of the farm boy, Hayseed. Larnie watched the two of them catch their horses, saddle up, and ride in the direction of the cowboys working the edges of the herd. She swallowed back a whimper of relief.

After a moment, Larnie turned to Buzzard. "You won't help me, either!"

He shook his head and snickered. "Them cowboys think you're one dumb female," was his answer. "So do I."

Larnie nodded, feeling nothing. She turned to study the thousands of cows — some grazing, some hooking horns in mock battle, others lying down chewing their cuds. The Hillyers' mare, Kate, was a good horse, smart, Larnie reasoned with herself. Kate had been rested, fed, and watered at the Wichita livery. The horse would know more about handling cows than a human being who had lived all her days in Leavenworth. She would trust Kate for the only help she was going to get.

Larnie mounted stiffly, hesitated, then kneed Kate toward the herd. "Hey!" she heard Buzzard protest after a moment. "What're you doin'? Don't — !"

She rode on. In her mind's eye she could see herself, as though one Larnie remained behind, the other advanced toward the dangerous herd. The Larnie on the horse was truly a sight. Her hair was loose, tangled under her awful bonnet. Her dress was torn and dirty. She was crying without sound, her tears making a hot, steady stream down her dusty cheeks. She didn't want to do what she was doing, didn't want to ride into a herd of watching, horn-rattling, red-eyed brutes. If there had been a choice, the Larnie on the horse would rather have been almost anywhere else in the world. If there had been a choice...

"Stop!"

Larnie glanced numbly in the direction of the command and saw a mixture of horror and admiration on Buzzard's face. Larnie turned back, lifted an arm, wiped at her eyes. She had to be able to see Bessie.

She was inside the big herd now. Curious cows ambled close, too close. The clatter and rattle of horns, the sounds of steamy snorts seemed to fill Larnie's ears, shutting out all other sounds. A strong cow smell, the smell of danger, filled her nose. Larnie stared at the cows, looking for the one she wanted — a short-horned brindle with a mark on her left shoulder. *Bessie*, she prayed, *let me see you.*

The cow brutes were pressing them, leaving no opening for escape. The occasional brindle Larnie spotted had those awful rocking-chair-long horns. Where was Bessie? She had to be here!

Larnie fully felt her own fear now. She pushed on, searching, scarcely able to breathe. To relieve the choked feeling in her throat, she reached up to loosen the knot in her bonnet strings. At that moment the wind picked up and lifted the bonnet, dead lilacs and all, from Larnie's fingers. The bonnet, caught in an eddying wind, whirled across the face of one cow, who instantly bolted. In less than a second, the entire herd was off in one thundering body, running hard, forcing Larnie on Kate to run with them.

For a moment Larnie was frozen with fear, then she bent low and threw her arms around Kate's neck. Oh, to be away from this nightmare, away, away, anywhere. Thick dust rose, filling her mouth and nose. Larnie closed her eyes against the world, which seemed to be turning upside down. Under her, the bay mare stumbled as cows pushed into them. There was a sudden searing pain in Larnie's left leg. No, oh, no... Larnie, hang on — hang on.

A soft, man's voice called her name. "Larnie! Hang on, kid, hang on!"

Through the din, Larnie heard. She tried to answer. Her voice was dead. It was over. She would die, like her voice. All of her would be gone, trampled under the running cows. They would never find her. I'm sorry, Mama, Papa, about the baby, about Bessie, about me, she cried silently. The Skitterbrain tried, but...

She could not hang on any longer. Larnie's fingers, grasping, struggling to hang on to Kate were torn free. Now? Would it happen now? No. No hooves crushed her body. She was going up, not down. The air was not so stifling. She was being lifted up. There was a firm band around her waist. An arm. From one bolting, rocking boat onto another. No, not a boat. A horse.

Larnie dared to open her eyes. She saw a leathery neck, an Adam's apple bobbing in it. Above that was a firm, whiskery jaw, a sandy mustache and unkempt sideburns, a brown temple where a blue vein stood out. It was Jeru Hunter. "Grab on to me," he muttered, "grab on." Larnie grabbed, then blacked out.

With a
Fine-Tooth Comb

As though from miles away, Larnie heard Buzzard's voice, thick with something in it, ask, "She hurt awful bad? Law, she was a brave 'un!"

"Knocked out, 's all. Her leg's been caught by a horn, not bad, though. Here, gimme the water. Let's get it cleaned. Find a clean rag. Ely, see if you can stop the bleeding. Why'd the kid do it? A wonder she wasn't killed! My herd is halfway back to Texas, I reckon! They gettin' 'em turned yet?" Even though Larnie's mind still wavered in a haze of dizziness, she could hear that Jeru Hunter was an angry as a hornet.

"Do you think she's loco?" Buzzard wanted to know.

"Why would a little girl ride smack into the middle of a bunch of longhorns?" Larnie recognized the concerned voice of Jeru Hunter's cook.

Her eyelids fluttered and she tried to make her numb lips move. They ought to ask *her*. She could tell them why she did it, had to do it. She'd been trying to tell them all along. "B-b-b-" It was the only sound she could make.

"Ho! She's coming around!"

"Raise her up. Let the poor little girl sit up."

"Get back, she needs air."

"What's she sayin'? Let 'er talk."

Larnie sat up, feeling sick to her stomach and hurting in every limb. She was on a pallet near the chuckwagon. Jeru Hunter was squatting close, one hand rubbing his own bad leg held out stiffly in front of him. Buzzard was also squatting, his eyes wide as he stared at her openmouthed. The bald cook, Ely, was gentle as he finished bandaging her leg.

Larnie struggled to speak through a dust-caked throat. "I — I saw my cow Bessie wander into your herd, Mr. Hunter, miles south of here, where I live with my papa and mama," she said, for what seemed the hundredth time. "I saw it happen myself," she whispered. "You have my cow. I've followed you, for days. I rode into your herd because you do have my cow—somewhere. I hope no one else was hurt, and I'm sorry about the stampede, but no one would help me."

The cook got to his feet and shaded his eyes.

"Looks like they got the herd slowed all right," he said. "They're milling. Didn't go so fur as they sometimes do. You and the rest of the crew got here from town just in time, boss."

Jeru Hunter's fingers kept running back through his thinning hair, although the anger in his eyes was dimming. "All right!" he said finally. He pounded a fist into the thick dust in front of him. "All right. I give up. I'll pay you for the cow right now, though I ain't got the money to spare. What'd your pa pay for it—ten, twenty dollars?"

Larnie rubbed her face with a dirty hand. Why didn't grownups ever listen? So often you told them something — something important — and they just didn't listen to what you were saying.

"Money won't feed a newborn baby, Mr. Hunter," she explained quietly. "My mother — Mama almost died last year. Our doctor in Leavenworth knew Mama was too frail to nurse our baby, so he made us buy a good milk cow to have when the baby came. I would take your money and buy another cow, but can you tell me where I can find a milk cow to buy, out here, in time?"

The trail boss's tan face turned beet-red. He looked away from Larnie's steady gaze. He got to his feet, slowly and with effort because of the bad leg. Exasperation and anger at the trouble she had caused still showed in Jeru Hunter's face. But he said, "I'll have my hands search the herd with a fine-tooth comb. Look for a brindle milk cow," he called to some of his men who were nearby. "Short-horned," he added sourly, "with a black crescent moon on its left shouder. God help me, and you, too, girl, if my herd stampedes again."

"Thank you," Larnie whispered, only half hearing his threat in her weary relief. "I know you'll find Bessie."

The cattle came back in wild-eyed straggling bunches, bringing a choking dust with them. It felt as if hours were passing while she waited, as the cowboys tried to locate Bessie among the rumbling herd. From where Larnie sat in the shade of the chuckwagon, she could hear some of the men singing softly as they rode back and forth through the hard-breathing, restless cows, looking for one brindled milk cow.

She could not see Buzzard anywhere, nor did he appear in the hour that followed.

With her heart in her throat, Larnie watched the riders gather for a talk some distance away. Then one of them rode forward to report to Jeru Hunter, who was soaking his leg with a hot pack not far from Larnie. "There ain't no milk cow in this herd, Mr. Hunter. Might have been lost in the stampede, but we don't think so. A farm cow wouldn't have run like these wild critters, she'd 'a' been the first one to stop. She ain't here."

Larnie shook her head in numb disbelief. If Bessie wasn't in the herd, what had happened to her? In a daze, Larnie saw the trail boss throw his hands in the air, heard him order his men back to work at whatever they'd been doing before Larnie interfered. He said nothing to Larnie, as though she was a bug too insignificant for further attention. To the cook, Ely, he said, "Will you wet this pack again? It helps this pesky leg a little. I'll sure be glad to get this herd sold," he ground out, "an' get back to Texas an' get me a rocking-chair job."

Larnie struggled to her feet and stood there, weaving. The cow camp had become a chillingly unfriendly place, where she didn't belong. She shook her head in an effort to think clearly, and looked toward the remuda. She saw that someone had caught Kate, the Hillyers' mare, and put her with the other spare horses. The mare didn't look any the worse for having been in the stampede except for sweat-shiny sides.

What had happened to Buzzard and Sunflower? She hadn't seen Buzzard since those first minutes after Jeru Hunter had rescued her and they'd all been talking at once as she came to If Buzzard wasn't going to let her take Papa's mule, she would have to make her way home on foot, after leaving Kate at the Hillyers'. There was little to do now but let Mama and Papa know that she had failed — predictably, a skitterbrain to the end. The trouble she had caused them was so serious that she would never be able to feel glad or happy again as long as she lived. The baby would surely...

"Gal! Larnie!" It was Buzzard pounding up on Sunflower, waving frantically at her. Buzzard reined the mule to a thudding halt. "Get on," he cried, "climb up behind me."

The look on Buzzard's grubby face made Larnie's spirits leap. She stumbled forward. "Bessie? Did you find her, Buzzard?"

"C'mon." He cackled with laughter. "Don't stand there sleepin'. Tarnation, gal, get on this mule!"

Larnie was astride behind Buzzard in seconds, her wounded leg, her despair forgotten. Although Sunflower carried double her usual load, the mule seemed to sense the mood of the two on her back, and she moved swiftly. Buzzard chortled with glee. Larnie laughed, too. She didn't question, because she *knew*. It was, it had to be.

After what seemed forever, some distance southeast of Hunter's cow camp, they arrived at a brushy draw. The spot would go unnoticed by most in a sweeping observation of the broad, flat plain. "In there," Buzzard said, pulling Sunflower to a halt.

Larnie was off the mule in a limping run, crashing down into the prickly brush. There stood Bessie, swishing her long tail against flies, her jaws rhythmically chewing her cud. "Bessie! There you are! Oh, you beautiful, beloved cow!" Larnie threw her arms around the cow's neck, smelled the green blossom smell that surrounded Bessie. She drew back to run a finger along one short golden horn and trace the black crescent moon on Bessie's left shoulder. Bessie let out a low moan of greeting and tossed her head. "We've found her at last, *you* found her — oh, Buzzard, how did she get here? How did you find Bessie?"

Buzzard flopped back to lay in the short grass on the bank of the draw, hands behind his head, grimy elbows in the air, and grinned broadly. "Used my head," he answered. "First I was just thinkin' about your cow, wonderin' if wherever she was somebody was milkin' her, cause cows can get plumb miserable if they ain't milked every day." He took a long breath. "Cowboys don't like milk, they likes their drinks to be of lots stronger stuff 'n milk. I didn't figure any of Jeru's cowboys would be havin' anythin' to do with your cow. Then I thunk. Hayseed! You know, Jeru's farmboy horse wrangler. He'd be tickled to see a milk cow caught in the herd, cause he'd be brought up on milk, like as not. Then I figured: Was I him, I'd hide the cow out. The other cowboys would make terrible fun of a milk-drinkin' cowhand."

Larnie was astonished. "I-I suppose it could be true!" She smiled and hugged Bessie again.

"Sure it is," Buzzard stated. "An' after I saw you ridin' into that herd, cryin' 'cause you were so awful scared but goin' just the same, I wanted to find your cow for you in the worst way. So I done me some thinkin' and figured it out, and went lookin' for your cow." He poked a dirty finger proudly at Bessie. "An' there she is."

"I thank you, Buzzard." Larnie smiled and swallowed back tears. "I really, really thank you." Her hand shook as she started to untie Bessie's lead rope from a hackberry limb. "I don't know how I'll ever thank you enough."

"I do. I'm goin' home with you!" Buzzard answered.

Larnie looked at him in surprise, a warm rush of feeling for the boy inside her. "Good. You know I want you to. But what made you change your mind?"

"I don't guess nobody ever did you such a good turn as findin' that cow for you," he bragged. "You owe me."

Larnie laughed. "You're right, Buzzard. But Papa really can use you on the farm, I know. The work — " A sound above them made Larnie look up.

Jeru Hunter sat his horse at the top of the draw. He nonchalantly rolled a cigarette as he watched them; his bothersome leg rested around the saddlehorn. He looked almost happy, too, that they had found Bessie, Larnie thought, but with such a face you couldn't be sure.

"I found out about this a few minutes ago," he said flatly. "Hayseed spotted the milk cow in our herd just before we got to Wichita. Hid her out in this draw and milked her on the sly. I had him busy workin' all the time, so he never did know you were here lookin' for the cow, until today," Jeru told Larnie.

"What are you going to do to him, Hayseed, your wrangler?" Larnie asked stiffly, her hands tight on Bessie's rope.

The trail boss let them wait a moment while he took a couple of drags on his cigarette. "Tastes like cowfeed," he said in sudden disgust, smashing the cigarette out on his saddlehorn. "What am I going to do about Hayseed?" he repeated, looking up. "Pin a medal on him, I reckon," he drawled. "Hayseed made a hero of himself turning the stampede you caused, girl. The boy is going to be a good cowhand someday. Like you" — he nodded at Buzzard — "if you don't give up."

Buzzard looked startled, then he beamed like a new day.

"We'll go back to camp for the Hillyers' mare," Larnie said, leading Bessie up the side of the draw, "then start right out for home."

"Whoa," Jeru Hunter said. "I know you ain't got no time to spare, but you two young'uns can't just light out alone on a thirty-mile trip with no grub or nothin'. You'll get there faster and easier if you are ready for it, so don't go off half-cocked. We'll get you a good meal under your belts, in town, me treatin', an' some extra oats for your animals, besides food to take for yourselves."

Larnie frowned. Jeru Hunter's plan seemed such a waste of time. Now that she had Bessie, she couldn't get home soon enough to suit her. Still, she didn't want to do things a skitterbrain's way, not ever again. "All right," she agreed reluctantly, "but can we hurry?"

Later, riding to town on three of Jeru Hunter's horses while Bessie, Kate, and Sunflower grazed and rested at camp, the trail boss explained, "I had to go into Wichita anyway. We been here a lot longer than we expected, waitin' for a decent deal for our cows. I think it's about settled, but Ely's low on supplies."

Larnie nodded, already knowing it to be true about the supplies. She had asked the cook to outfit them so they wouldn't have to go into Wichita, but he'd shown her his empty barrels and boxes.

At the center of town they found a greater commotion than usual, even for Wichita. The air was filled with the sound of booted feet running along the boardwalks. Sharp men's voices called to one another. Groups of men were making quick noisy knots in the street, and a long line of men began to form in front of a vacant shack.

"What's going on?" Jeru Hunter asked a passerby.

Larnie saw the man's head, in a sweat-stained Stetson, motion. "That feller, yonder," the man told them, "has stole from folks in this town long enough. Folks are decidin' what to do with him, in an interestin' way for Wichita."

Because of her anxiety to be going home, Larnie was hardly interested, but when she glanced across the street at the man seated on the ground, tightly bound with rope to a hitching post, a soft cry of surprise escaped her. It was the odd-looking man who had followed her. Tom McGrath! His oversized gray hat was gone, and she saw that the hair on his head was as red as his beard and equally unkempt.

The passerby was saying, "In that empty shack

they got a table with a hat on it, and two sacks of beans. We're votin' one by one. We go in, drop a white bean in the hat if we think McGrath ought to be hanged, a red bean in the hat if we think he'll learn his lesson by bein' run out of town on a rail. When we're done they'll count the beans to see —"

In that instant the red-whiskered captive spotted Larnie. His head jerked up, he strained at his ropes but couldn't move. "Gal," he shouted hoarsely. "Larnie. That's you. Come over here, quick, I got to tell you — !"

"Do you know him?" Jeru Hunter grunted at Larnie.

Her heart beat fast. Larnie shook her head. "No. Not really. I — I don't think so. But he knows my name, somehow."

"We ought to find out what the gent wants, don't you figure?" Buzzard looked eager to talk to the captive outlaw.

"Unh," Jeru Hunter grunted.

"No, I must hurry," Larnie protested, but Jeru Hunter and Buzzard were aiming their mounts toward the bound man on the opposite side of the street. Larnie sighed and urged her own horse to follow.

"You got something on your mind, mister?" Jeru Hunter asked.

"Yeh, do you?" Buzzard echoed.

Larnie said nothing. How could anything this thief might have to say be of interest to her? She wanted to go home. Larnie twisted impatiently in the saddle, her glance on the road out of town. Tom McGrath spoke suddenly, and Larnie's spine stiffened. She turned slowly to look down at the sweating man.

"Your pa sent me, girl. I was coming back from Indian Territory, where I took some" — the man hesitated, shrugged — "some goods to sell. Come by your pa's place and stopped for a drink of water from your well. Came right into some trouble at your house. Your mama."

Icy fingers climbed up Larnie's spine. Speechless, she begged with a look for McGrath to go on.

"Your pa couldn't leave your mama to go looking for you. He told me you took off after a stray cow and hadn't come back. Your pa's a good man. He give me some money to find you and bring you home. As you can see, I done found you but I can't take you back to your folks. Tell your pa I'm sorry I got the job only half done."

Larnie shook her head frantically. "It — it doesn't matter. My — my mama? Is she...is she...? Is the baby...?"

McGrath nodded his grizzled head gravely. "The babe hadn't come yet. There was some trouble. . . . I wish you and your folks all the best, miss. I'm sorry I — "

There was a blur before Larnie's eyes and a painful lump in her throat. She swallowed and waved McGrath silent. "Thank you for telling me." Larnie turned toward Jeru Hunter. "I want to start home, right now."

Jeru Hunter's eyes, turned on Larnie, were kind, his voice husky as he answered, "We'll forget the meal here, just grab a few supplies at the general store for you to have on the way. No use to get yourself worked up, Larnie, you're not going to get there any faster than you can push that milk cow, anyhow. You probably won't — "

The trail boss didn't finish but Larnie knew what he was thinking: that they wouldn't make it in time, anyway. Oh, but they would, she thought. She clamped her jaws tight to stop the quivering and lifted her face. Oh, yes, they would.

Going Home

Inside the general store, Larnie rushed around grabbing the items Jeru Hunter insisted that she and Buzzard take with them. While Jeru counted out some coins, the grocer stuffed the loaf of bread, beefjerky, dried peaches, and matches in the gunnysack the trail boss handed him.

"Is that it, are we ready?" Larnie asked anxiously. Jeru Hunter grunted.

They rode hard the two miles to the cow camp. At the camp Larnie and Buzzard would change from Jeru's horses to Kate and Sunflower, and take Bessie in tow. On top of her own worry, Larnie could see that Buzzard was preoccupied about something other, she believed, than her mission.

He asked her at last, "D'you think they'll hang that red-haired gent back there? I wish we could have stayed for the countin' of the beans."

"He isn't a bad man, not all bad, anyway," Larnie said. "I'm sure it will be red beans for sending him away. I should have known, when he was following me in Wichita." She shrugged and fell silent, her mind unable to stay long on a subject other than her mother and the baby. Thirty miles was such a long, long way, with a cow to lead, or drive.

"How long do you think it will take us?" Larnie asked back at camp as they readied their animals for the trip. The bay mare and Sunflower looked refreshed, and raring for a job to do. Larnie wasn't so sure about the tethered Bessie, who stood with her eyes closed, lazily chewing her cud.

"Keep your animals movin'," Jeru Hunter answered as he tightened Kate's cinch. "Stay on 'em, but let 'em graze now and then, water 'em every chance you get. If you don't have any trouble that'll slow you down, you can make it" — he squinted thoughtfully at the sky — "by tomorrow night. Or the morning after."

Although she couldn't have said when it happened, Larnie realized she had come to feel a liking for the stocky cowboy. He had helped her more than he needed to. Maybe, if he didn't have the bad leg, and if he weren't in a job he plainly didn't care for, Mr. Hunter could be a very nice person, Larnie thought. "Thank you. For everything," she warmly told him.

The gaze he turned on her was level, serious. "I'd give anything if I had listened to you when you first came to me about your cow." He shook his head. "I would send one of my men along with you, but they wouldn't be able to get you home any faster than you can get there yourselves. Ain't no use to travel at night," he advised, "you'll just get lost and go off in the wrong direction."

Larnie smiled her thanks. Buzzard, in one longing look, took in the camp, the cowboys, and the cattle before he leaped astride Sunflower. Kate's saddle creaked as Larnie climbed aboard. Jeru Hunter handed Bessie's rope to Larnie, and they were moving in the direction of home at last. There were several shouts of "good luck" from the cowboys behind them.

Larnie looked apprehensively at the endless miles of prairie spread before them. It was good that they had several hours of daylight left to travel in today.

They rode in silence, facing into the southwind, for a long time. Later, Larnie felt no fear when they spotted the buffalo herd about a mile west of the trail. She watched them grazing under a deep-blue sky, in the waving green-brown grass, and knew what majestic creatures the buffalo truly were.

It was Buzzard who spoke, finally. "I never thought I'd see a *gal* do something like you did, ride right into that herd of mean old longhorns," he said admiringly, grinning. "You know, I don't think I'd have done it. But," he added quickly, sending Sunflower on faster with his heels, "I might have."

"In a way what I did was stupid," Larnie told him. "But if you had been me, I think you would have gone into that herd to look for Bessie. There are times when we don't have a choice. Anyway, we have to face up to our troubles with gumption, make good of the mistakes we — " Larnie broke off, surprised. She'd been using Papa's words, almost exactly. She smiled to herself and her heart went out to Papa, so far ahead, doing for Mama in her trouble.

Again they rode in silence, the anxious hours passing slowly. In the west the sun was setting, and Larnie knew that with full dark they should stop for the night, give their animals a rest.

After a while, she turned Kate southwest toward the wild woman's dugout, and motioned for Buzzard to follow on Sunflower. When the woman came out of the dugout to greet them, Buzzard's eyes nearly popped out of his head. "She's a friend," Larnie whispered. The lonely woman, smiling and chattering, led the youngsters and their animals to a well and trough behind the dugout. Larnie made certain Bessie was tethered securely. She unsaddled Kate, and gave the three animals some of the oats Jeru Hunter had sent with them.

After a supper of buffalo steak and Bessie's milk, Larnie and the woman talked in the dimness of the dugout, reassuring, friendly woman talk that made a bond between the older woman and the young girl.

Buzzard insisted on sleeping outside with their stock, and he confided to Larnie in a hiss that he would not close his eyes all night, he was so fearful of the "witch." "She's not!" Larnie protested, in vain.

They made ready to leave next morning while the moon was high and dawn had not yet come. Larnie promised the woman, "If the baby — when the baby is old enough to travel, we will bring him to visit you."

The woman in black, her arms cuddling emptiness, took a step after them. "I can hold him?" she asked, her face glowing. "I can hold the baby?"

"Of course," Larnie said with a smile.

"If you're careful," Buzzard muttered.

They faced the wide empty horizon and rode steadily south. At the Hillyers' homestead, Larnie had to part with the mare, Kate, that she'd come to love and appreciate so much.

Ma Hillyer had been delighted to see her, Larnie remembered, as she and Buzzard continued on their way. The sons, Luke and John, were surprised but pleased that she had found her Bessie after all. Buzzard had had to endure a passel of teasing for the trick he had played on them all. No one spoke of what Larnie might find at home, but the Hillyers' farewell handclasps were warm and tight, and their eyes granted her more good wishes than could ever be spoken aloud.

Larnie's eyes grew misty as she remembered. She could scarcely see the dusty, hoof-imprinted trail that stretched into seeming infinity before them. Now that Sunflower no longer limped, she and Buzzard rode double, Larnie in front, with Bessie's lead rope held fast in her hand.

They covered mile after mile with such wretched slowness that at times Larnie felt she could not bear it. Time dragged, and it was as though they were on a treadmill, going nowhere. Only her yearning desperation seemed to be moving, going on ahead by leaps and bounds.

At Cowskin Creek they rested and watered the animals. Larnie was too tired to have an appetite, but she ate the beefjerky and bread for the strength they would give her. She chewed with difficulty, staring out on the muddy brown water. Maybe, if she didn't think so much about home, they would seem to get there faster, she told herself. Suddenly, without warning, a feeling of sadness struck her, a feeling so overwhelming, so sharp that Larnie's mind went blank. Home was all that mattered, and home was wherever Mama and Papa and the new baby were. She jumped to her feet. "We must go," she said chokingly, "let's hurry." She felt Buzzard's eyes on her, but he said nothing.

Hours passed. Late in the day the wind picked up and began to howl like a living animal. Walking now, Larnie touched her face, and it was cool under her fingertips. Dark rolling clouds were advancing from the west. Within minutes, Larnie's dress was being whipped about her body. Hail as large as bullets and almost as painful beat down. "We've got to keep going," she yelled at Buzzard above the roar of the wind. "Don't stop."

"Yeh!" he yelled. "I won't. But this hail feels like wasps are stingin' me all over. This here mule is givin' me a time. Don't let that cow get loose from you," he warned. "Not now!"

"I won't."

An hour of pouring rain followed. Then, as suddenly as it began, the storm ended. A warm dazzling sun broke through the clouds, sending steam up from the earth.

"Over," Larnie was able to say. "We'll make it."

"Yeh."

They had covered many miles without really

being aware of their heartbreaking pace, Larnie realized, thanks to the distraction of the weather.

Close to dusk, they came to the Ninnescah River and the cottonwood where the two of them had spent that first night hating each other. Larnie and Buzzard exchanged looks, remembering without words. In weary silence they cared for their animals and ate the last of the food. In the trees nearby, a turtledove cooed mournfully.

"Do you want to try to make it all the way home tonight?" Buzzard asked with a look that said he hoped she wouldn't, but if she did, he would go, too.

Larnie nodded. "We'll have moonlight later, to see the trail by."

In grueling, mindless silence, they covered the last miles, again riding double on the plodding mule. Larnie hung on to Bessie's lead rope as though it were life itself. When night fell, they didn't stop, although Sunflower was moving so slowly that Buzzard decided to walk.

The moon came up. Larnie was aware that Buzzard's steps were wooden, faltering beside her. They must keep going. She was sure they must be close, now. Larnie fought to keep her head up, her eyes open. She took a couple of turns around her wrist with Bessie's lead rope, just in case.

Eternities later, it seemed, Larnie thought she saw in a wash of moonlight dark lumps in front of them. Home? She stared hard. "Look," she whispered hoarsely, "look, Buzzard, that's our place, ahead there." Evidently perceiving that they, too, were near their old home, their destination, Sunflower, under her, and Bessie following, moved faster.

"That's it, huh?" Buzzard asked in a tired but happy voice, running to catch up.

As they grew nearer, Larnie saw through filmy burning eyes that Papa had his windmill up. She could see it by the light of the moon and hear it whirring in the south wind. A dim light glowed through the greased paper covering the single window of the little sod house, even this late at night.

She was stiff and sore all over when she climbed down from Sunflower's back. Only then did she turn Bessie's rope over to Buzzard. "We're here." She walked alone to the sod house and opened the door. Across the room, Papa sat in the lamplight by Mama's bed; a soft mewing sound came from a bundle beside Mama's thin, quilt-covered form.

"How are they?" Larnie asked. "I've brought Bessie, she's outside." Papa looked up. He stared at Larnie as though he didn't dare believe his eyes. Then he was across the room, clasping her in his arms, his cheek suddenly wet as he pressed it down to hers. Larnie clung to him. "Papa, I'm so glad to be home. Please, how's Mama? How's the baby?"

"All right," he said huskily against her ear. "We are all just fine, now."

"Dumpling?" came a whisper from across the room, so faint Larnie could scarcely hear it. "My Larnie, is that you? Oh, Larned!"

Papa released her and Larnie moved quickly to the bed. "I'm home, Mama. I'll tell you everything, later." She kissed Mama's forehead. "I brought Bessie. The baby...?"

Mama's trembling hand reached to turn back a corner of the soft blanket under her arm. "Your little brother, Larnie. His name is Carson."

"Oh," Larnie whispered, "oh, he is so tiny. But he is...?"

"Very hungry," Mama said. "He's cried himself out with hunger. We've kept him alive these two days since he was born with sugar water, but he needs milk. You've brought Bessie just in time."

"If somebody'd git me a bucket," a brusque boy's voice said suddenly from the doorway, "I'd milk." Mama and Papa looked startled at sight of the bedraggled young boy who struggled to hold Bessie back from coming into the house.

Papa looked at Larnie. She smiled. "This is a friend I've found who needs a good home," she explained. "He'll help us with all our work on the farm. Mama, Papa, meet — meet John."

Buzzard gaped at first, then his grubby face melted into an unbelievably happy grin. He took Papa's hand and shook it. "Pleased to meet you, Larnie's Papa."

"Welcome, John," Papa said. "We sure can use you, Johnny." He gave the boy's shoulders a shake of gratitude that made Buzzard beam.

"Here, B-Johnny, take the milk bucket," Larnie said, snatching it up from the wash bench inside the door. "Our baby brother is starving."

With Papa and the newly named Johnny outside, busy with Bessie, Larnie turned and tiptoed back to the bed. Mama had fallen asleep, relief written all over her thin face. The baby stirred weakly, and Larnie reached out a hand to lay it on the bundle, comforting the tiny creature. "There, there," she whispered. "I've come home. Everything will be better now."